PAST ALL DISHONOR

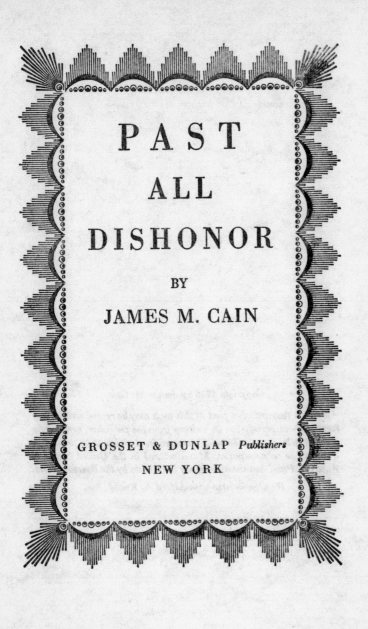

PAST
ALL
DISHONOR

BY

JAMES M. CAIN

GROSSET & DUNLAP *Publishers*

NEW YORK

This book deals with the West of the silver boom, and the amateur of that era will find much in it which is familiar to him. The characters, however, are imaginary, as are the specific mines, establishments, and intrigues that engage them. They do not represent, and are not intended to represent, actual persons, places, or events, nor do they spring from local legend, directly or under disguise.

J. M. C.

PAST ALL DISHONOR

 1

I first met her, this girl you'll find soon enough, when she fished me out of the Sacramento River on an occasion when I was showing more originality than sense. I was taking a day off from my job, which was secesh spy, though I may as well say right away there was no bravery attached to it, or anything like what they put in the novels. Last year, when Lee got kicked out of Maryland, I figured it was time to quit griping at how the feds ruined Annapolis, and do something about it. So I was packed for Port Tobacco, where I was to cross into Virginia and enlist, when a friend of mine heard something that scared him worse than what had happened to Lee. He's got a big statehouse job, and gets a lot of stuff not everybody gets. And he heard

about the Column from California, as they called
it, that crossed the Colorado and moved through
Arizona and New Mexico into Texas, and when
we laid it out on the map it looked like they were
going to scoop the Confederacy right into the Gulf
of Mexico like a scythe scoops wheat. So he got a
bunch together, and they had it all night, and decided there was still a chance for the western republic idea, but that our trouble was we didn't
know anything about California. So I got elected
to go out there and send news back. But right away
they warned me not to send any military informa-
tion, unless it was hot and important, in which case
I was to wire in a simple code we had that wouldn't
be suspected. Mainly I was to send newspaper clippings, and as Sacramento was a central spot, specially for political stuff, I settled down there, and
took a shack by the river, on the Yolo side, so I
could use a glass on the boats and anything else I
wanted to see without anybody asking why. Couple
of days a week I rockered a placer up on the American River, so there couldn't be any question about
what I was doing there. As a matter of fact I got
enough color to live on. About once a week I'd take

2

a steamboat trip up one of the rivers, to see what was going on, and there's been plenty. That independent republic may not be such a dream as you'd think. And every couple of days I'd send on my clippings, covering both sides, like I was just a young fellow keeping his friends back east up to date. On the wire part, there wasn't much to send. California is not where the war is, and even in San Francisco, outside of training new outfits going east, there's not much military news.

One day in spring it got hot, and I put on some trunks and went in the river. The Sacramento, it's not any Severn, but it felt good just the same and I fooled around quite a while. Then a boat came in and I swam over for her wash. Then I decided to board her for a dive. Her bumpers were out, and by pulling up on her wheel I could catch one and go over the rail of the freight deck. But I had forgotten how they do on these river boats. They hit the pier like they hit it, put out a plank to let off passengers, and then later they snug in for the day. So when that wheel began to turn, it was bad news. All hands were wharfside, and nobody was there to hear me holler and maybe tell the engineer. I

hung on for a second, but that was taking me right
up in the box. I dropped, and that put me at the
bottom of the river, with mud swirling all around
me, and that wheel overtop of me hooking it up like
a thunderstorm.

How long I was down there I don't know, and if
a blade clipped me I couldn't be sure. Next thing
I knew I was coming up, and my head was out, but
I couldn't breathe on account of the foam all
around, smothering me. Then something hit me on
the head and I grabbed it. It was a fire bucket, the
kind that's made of canvas, with a rope on it, that
they heave into the river when they want water
quick. I hung on, and got some air, and caught sight
of her, but whether she was young or old or pretty
or plain I didn't notice. She tied the bucket to the
section of rail that goes over the hatch, and
stretched her hand down to me. It didn't reach. She
threw both legs over the rail, turned around with
her back to the river, dropped a foot down, and
told me to catch hold of it. I did, and then inch by
inch I went up. Each time she'd pull, a little noise
would come out of her mouth, but it had guts to it
and I knew if I could just hold on she'd get me out.

4

DISHONOR

Then I caught the deck, and then we were on the rail. After I got my breath back, I began to notice what she looked like. She was around medium height, but seemed taller because she was so slim. She had on a black silk dress with white dots, but with no hoops in it, and you could see what a soft willowy shape she had. She had a pale skin, black hair, and thick red lips. She was plenty good-looking. "Well say, that was pretty nice of you. Thanks."

"That all the sense you've got? Fooling around a place that any couter would know enough to keep away from?"

"I craved me a dive."

"You got one all right. You know what's good for you you'll go back where you come from and quit getting yourself in a mess somebody else has to pull you out of."

"I still crave me a dive."

"Then you still got no sense."

I went up to the passenger deck, then on up to the texas deck, and straightened up for my dive. But then my head began pounding and that water looked an awful way down. Then I fell against the

5

texas, and then I was down on the passenger deck
again, holding on to the rail to keep from falling
into the river. On the other side of the boat they
were rolling freight, and she was down there on the
freight deck, at the foot of the stairs. It crossed my
mind, what was she doing there, when all other passengers had gone ashore? Then she happened to
look up, and came racing up to where I was. She
put her arm around me, took me in the main saloon,
and from there into a stateroom, and sat me down.

But my teeth started to chatter, and I thought if
I didn't get warm I'd die. She got a towel and
rubbed me off dry. Then a blanket was around me
and she was helping me to the bed. Then I was
under the covers and that was all I knew for a
while.

When I woke up it was dark and a lot of talk was
going on outside the door. Pretty soon I began to
listen, and it seemed to be between the boat captain,
a deputy, and some woman that claimed she was
robbed. "It was just an ordinary black pocketbook
with a strap across the back for my fingers, but it

contained all my worldly goods, twenty-six double eagle pieces, four dollars in silver, two cents in copper, my wedding certificate, and a lock of my boy's hair that went in the army."

"Where did you miss this here pocketbook?"

"At Rio Vista."

"Not after they pulled out from Rio Vista?"

"Mr. Deputy, can't I read? We were tied up at Rio Vista wharf with the sign looking me right in the face. I was watching the people come aboard, and my heart almost stopped when I realized I didn't have my pocketbook. By the look on this girl's face I knew she took it, and right away I went to the captain."

"But it was Rio Vista?"

"How many times have I got to tell you?"

"Then it's a Solano County case."

"It's—what?"

"It has to be handled by Solano County, not Sacramento County. I take her to Rio Vista, you go with me, I turn her over to the Solano County officers, and they hold her for the grand jury. The grand jury hears you, returns an indictment if the evidence warrants it, and the case is tried."

"They hear *me?*"

"You're the one that lost the pocketbook."

"When do you take me back?"

"Now. Tonight."

"Why can't she be searched now and I get my pocketbook back and that's all I want anyhow without me having to go clear on back to Rio Vista?"

"Did you explain her that, captain?"

"I've explained it till I'm tired. Madame, they got laws in this country and nobody gets searched on my boat till they're under arrest and I see the papers. This company is not taking chances on a case that rests on the look somebody has got on their face. Did you ever see the look on your face?"

"I say she took it."

"Then charge her."

She didn't answer, and the captain said: "Madame, will you kindly make up your mind one way or the other, so I can get out of here like I was supposed to do three hours ago? We've been all afternoon fooling around with you, looking up officers and neglecting everything else, and I ask you, for God's sake, will you kindly hatch a chicken or get the hell off the nest?"

8

"You stop talking to me like that."

"Then say something."

"If I charge her do they search?"

"And haul you back."

"I charge her."

It was up to me to get out, because a nearly naked man in her bed wasn't doing her any good. I opened the door on a crack and looked, but they were all over the saloon, not only the girl, the captain, the deputy, and the woman, but twenty or thirty passengers with drinks in their hands listening. I closed the door and went to the window. Nobody was out there, but it was so small I wondered if I would get stuck, like a pig under a gate. But it was my only chance, so I stuck my head out, got an arm through, and commenced to squirm. I'm six feet three, but I thought I had grown to eight yards from the skin I left on that sill and the rip I gave one leg, where it swung against a raw screw that was sticking out of one of the bedposts where the knob was missing. Finally I was out, and I wasn't one second too soon, because when my rump hit the deck a light showed, and when I raised up to peep they were in there.

They went through her trunk and the pillows on

the bed and the mattress and bedclothes, and then
the deputy said: "Very well, young woman, I'll
leave you here with the maid, and deputize her to
search your person."

Then the men went out, and the maid stepped
over to search. She was a big blonde girl that looked
like a Swede. And the woman that lost the pocketbook stepped over to watch, her lips pulled in and
her chin pushed out, and the breath whistling
through her nose. But then my heart gave a bump.
Because the way those black eyes were narrowed
down to two little slits, and the way those thick red
lips were twisted up, I knew there wasn't going to
be any searching, not by this pair. The maid knew
it too, because she backed off and began to chatter
something about her not being responsible in any
way, she was just deputized by the officer. And the
woman knew it too, when that smack hit one side of
her face like a pistol shot, and the curls were jerked
off the other side so hard the hat and wig came with
them, and she standing there screaming, as bald as
a coot. When the deputy came in with the captain
and some men, he backed off from those hard eyes
too. "And maybe you think you can search me?"

"Miss, I'm not required to use force, and I've no intention of doing it. I'm required to warn you, however, that whatever you say and do can be used against you, and if you refuse to submit to search, that fact will no doubt be most interesting to a jury. Beyond denying you the freedom of the boat, which I had intended to give you, and locking you in this stateroom, I won't go into the matter any further."

"You mean you can't."

"Have it any way you like, miss."

"But *he* can."

She walked over to the captain, switching her hips. "Because he's pretty. And because I can't have things used against me. Because I'se pretty too, and can't have myself put in any jail." She raised her hands above her head and looked up at him. It was the first I had seen her smile, and I hated it she was smiling at him, not me, and letting him feel all over her breasts and hips and legs, and even lifting her dresses so he could search her better. Outside, the passengers were laughing and yelling dirty stuff, and every word a stab into my heart, that had been beating so hard before because I was proud of her. At last it was done, and they were all gone, except

11

that the captain looked her in the eye on his way out, and said he'd drop by if he had time, and she said please do. I thought I ought to say good-bye to her, and thank her for saving my life, but couldn't make myself do it. I slunk down the stairs to the freight deck, and went over the side the way I came aboard, and swum across to the shack.

I was climbing out on my little plank landing before I felt that throb in my throat. Because there was my boat, the oars tucked under the seats, and all I had to do was jump in and I'd be alongside that steamer in a minute. I think I did it in half a minute. I threw the painter over the same rail she had used for the bucket, vaulted over to the freight deck, and ran up the stairs. Nobody noticed me that I could see. The deckhands were all in the bow, rolling freight off the pier, and the passengers were at the rail watching them, or else in the bar, having a drink. She was lying down, reading a paper, when I called, but she jumped up and came to the window. "I was wondering where you'd got to."

"I've been getting my boat. Come on. Hurry."

She dragged her trunk over, and I lifted it out

the window. It was one of those little leather ones that fit nice in the stagecoaches. Then she got her black cape and I took it, and leaned out the window so I could pull her through. We slipped down the stairway and I helped her in the boat. As I lowered the trunk, a bell rang in the engine room. It seemed a year before I could cast off the painter, grab the oars, and dig. As I shot away, the wheel began to turn. I was headed upstream, because the current had swung me that way, but I didn't take time to turn. I kept on going, past the steamer's bow, and shot under the next pier. She was in the stern, but now she moved up beside me, and we sat there, and held our breath, and watched. The steamer was pointed upstream too, because they always come in against the current, and she kept on that way until she was pretty close to the bridge. Then a hawser lifted out of the water, and you could hear the deck-hands grunt as they began pulling it in. She came around till we could almost have touched her, then she was pointed downriver, and the wharfmaster threw the hawser off the piling, and another bell rang in the engine room. We got some spray in our faces, and almost before you could believe it there was nothing but lights going downriver while the band played *Oh! Susanna.*

We laughed. Then we laughed again, and I put my arm around her and she let me. Then she came close and kissed me and I kissed back and I knew I loved her and she had to be mine.

2

"What do I do now?"

"Your family live here?"

"My family's dead."

"Where did you figure to go from the boat?"

"To a hotel."

"You can't do that now. They'll be looking for you."

"What you trembling about?"

"I got a shack."

"Must be cold there, the way you shake."

"You could come in there."

"With you?"

"It's not much, but you'd be hidden."

"What's your name?"

"Roger. Roger Duval."

"You from Louisiana?"

"The name's French, but I'm from Maryland."

"Morina's my name. Morina Crockett."

"You talk like Louisiana."

"I was born in Mobile, but I lived in New Orleans."

"How old are you?"

"Twenty-three. How old are you?"

"Twenty-one."

"My little piece of live bait, with blue eyes and curly gold hair, that I pulled out of the river. Roger, when I get a little *bitty* shrimp, I like to hold him in my hand, just to feel him wiggle. Suppose I get to wondering how *you'd* feel wiggling?"

"Then you're coming?"

"I'm a coon up a tree. What else can I do?"

She moved over to the stern, and leaned back on both hands while I pulled across the river, and kept looking at me, her eyes big and black in the starlight, and just a little bit it seemed they were laughing at me. At the landing I stood up to help her out, but she kept sitting there, and then: "Roger, could I borrow your boat?"

". . . What for?"

"Something I got to do."

"Well, can't I do it for you?"

"It's kind of private."

I stood there figuring, and all of a sudden it hit me that if she could handle a boat and pull up the next landing, that would kind of take care of everything she had to worry about, specially as it was on the Yolo side and there would be no Sacramento officers to be looking for her. I must have sounded pretty sulky: "Take it, then. Will you drop me a note where you leave it? So I can come get it? It handles nice and I kind of like it. Roger Duval, care general delivery, Sacramento, Calif."

"I bet you wiggle nice."

"And watch the oarlocks. They're loose."

"Aren't you taking my trunk out? . . . You're the cutest thing I ever saw in my life, and I'm not leaving you. But I got a use for this boat."

Then I saw, or thought I saw, that it had something to do with the ladies' promenade, and wanted to tell her I was pretty well fixed in that line back of the shack, but you can't say a thing like that, so I just stooped down to pick up her trunk. She put her hand over my lips. "Wiggle your mouth."

I kissed the inside of her fingers, and then she kissed me all over the face and I stepped out with the trunk. She moved over to the seat and picked up the oars, and as soon as she pushed off from the landing I saw she had handled plenty of boats. I ran up to the shack and got some clothes on at last and lit a fire in the front room and some charcoal in the kitchen. But even before that I went in the bedroom, ripped the blankets off the bed, and made it up again with sheets. I had some, as well as some pillow cases, my aunt had packed when I left. A fellow in a shack, he don't bother with them, but I was glad I had them, and that they were clean. Then I went on back and began skinning the rabbit I had bought that morning, and cleaning it, and cutting it up for the fire.

I was peeling the potatoes before it came to me she'd been gone one hell of a time. I went out front and looked, and all you could see was the lights of the water front, and all you could hear was the banjos in the bars, and the splash of somebody diving in the river. It was the dismalest sound you

18

ever heard, first the tinkle of the music with the whooping in between, then every few minutes this splash. I walked up and down, afraid she'd got stuck on a bar, then I went down to the next fellow's landing, thinking maybe she'd come to the wrong place. But his boat was there and mine wasn't. Then coming back I started to run, because something was moving on the river. And then sure enough there she was, just coming in to my landing. "Did you think I was never coming?"

"I was afraid something had happened to you."

"I've been doing something crazy."

"Go on up where it's warm. We're ready to eat."

"I could eat a whole possum."

She ran up the path, and I paddled the boat out to the stake. I made the stern fast, but when I started for the bow something rolled under my feet. It was a little white knob, with a neck on it and three or four feet of string. I picked it up and saw it was the missing knob from that bedpost, the one that had the screw sticking out that raked my leg. And then it came to me in a flash, what until then hadn't even entered my mind. She took the pocketbook. It was her diving for it into the river. And

19

this thing was the marker she had to have, when she threw it overboard, that would float up a few feet when that gold sank in the mud, and show where it was if she ever had the chance to go down and get it.

She was kneeling in front of the fireplace when I came back, the trunk open beside her, combing her hair over her face to dry it. "Guess what I did."

". . . Fell overboard?"

"I took me a bath."

"Where?"

"In the river."

"I've got a tank and sprinkler."

"I wish I'd known. But I'm so dirty from traveling that I just felt awful. I knew my little shrimp was all washed up, and I couldn't come in here unless I was as clean as he was."

I was behind her, and she gave my leg a pat, and I was just opening my mouth to say she wasn't coming in here or anywhere until she handed over that money and we figured a way to send it back. But just then she lifted her head and began combing in the opposite direction, and a big swatch of her hair hit me in the face, soft and warm and heavy, then went slipping down over my hands to the floor, and a clutch came in my throat so nothing would come out of it. "Did you say we're going to eat?"

". . . Yes, I'll—get busy."

I had taken the rabbit off the fire when I went out looking for her, but I had left the potatoes half on, and they were boiling now, so I put the rabbit back, and set a pot of beans up there to heat, and she came out to keep me company, braiding her hair in one thick snaky coil that she kept throwing around my head like a lasso while I was digging into the beans with a spoon to keep them from burning. "Got a skillet?"

"There's one under the coffee pot."

"I'll cook those beans."

She took up the beans with the spoon, patted them into little cakes, and fried out a little bacon grease. Then she put in the bean cakes and fried them up brown. By then the rabbit and potatoes were ready, and I got to say those beans were pretty good. Come to find out, she didn't learn that trick in New Orleans at all, but in Caracas, where she lived the last couple of years before she came west. "What did you do there?"

"Oh, this and that."

"What you doing here, Morina?"

"Oh, these and those."

"Of course, it's not really my business."

"I'm doing you, that's my business."

She was leaning close, over the little kitchen table I had back there, biting at a leg of rabbit with her big white teeth, and getting her cheek a little greasy down near the chin, and I thought of a way to get back to the money again, by saying "the business you got before any other business is to let me send back that money or do it yourself." But instead I said: "There's a jug of wine in that bin there, but all we got to drink it out of is tin cups."

"Oh you've got something else, haven't you?"

"No, I'm sorry."

"How much you want to bet?"

". . . A night's bed and board."

"Bring on the wine."

I got out the jug, a gallon jug with a big cork in it. She threw it over one shoulder, pulled the cork out with her teeth, then rocked it a couple of times to listen how much was in it. It was about half full. Then all of a sudden she fell on one knee and give

22

it a jerk, and the wine poured in her mouth like a hose was doing it. Her throat throbbed like a canary bird's does, and the wine gurgled down it for three or four seconds. Then she snapped the jug up again, swallowed three or four times, gasped, and said: "Did I spill any?"

"Not a drop."

"Don't I win?"

"I owe you a night's bed and board."

We went in and sat by the fire. "Does my shrimp smoke?"

"Not out here. The tobacco's bad."

"Wait."

She got out a little green package of black *cigarrillos*, she called them, gave me one and took one herself. "*You* smoke?"

"Course I smoke."

"That's new to me."

"Maybe a lot of things are new to you."

She blew smoke in my eyes. I puffed my *cigarrillo* but I didn't inhale it, because it was thick, white, sweet smoke I was afraid would make me sick. Mixed with the wine it just made me lazy. She kept blowing smoke in my mouth, looping her hair around my neck, and looking at me through the smoke. I put my arm around her, pulled her to me, and pushed my mouth up against hers. Then we were stretched out on the bearskin, the fire just a red glow all over the room, our faces hot, looking into each other's eyes. I knew then I wasn't going to say anything about the money that night, and that I wasn't ever going to do it.

Next morning I woke up wondering if any of it was true, but I looked over and her black braid of hair was looped all over the pillow, and the blankets went up and down with her breathing, though she was so slim you could hardly see anybody was there. I didn't make any move, but pretty soon a hand slid over and touched my hand, and I put my arms around her and we lay there a long time with the sleepy smell all around us. "I say what let's do today."

"What we going to do, live bait?"

"Go on a picnic."

"Fried chicken picnic?"

"Fried chicken picnic and catch fish."

"That sounds all right."

After we fried up some eggs and ate them for breakfast I got in the boat and crossed over to the water front and got a chicken and some more eggs and other stuff. Then I cut off the chicken's head and we picked him and fried him and boiled up the eggs and peeled them and packed all that and some bread and butter and fruit in a basket, and started out. I put some fishing lines in and a couple of miles down I threw out the anchor and we baited up with some worms I had dug the week before and put down our lines. It was one of those days you get once in six months. Everything was biting, from cats to perch, and we must have pulled in two dozen fish before we decided it was time to quit. It's bare country down there, with mud flats all around, and no woods or anything, but here and there is a green grove of willow trees right down to the water's edge. We shoved in there and went ashore, and there was an old hulk of a sailboat not far off, that had some short timbers in her I could prize off with the anchor prong, and in a few minutes we had a fire going and were broiling fish and getting out our other stuff, but saving our chicken for tonight. Then we lay on the bank and talked about the war. I hinted around I was for the South, to see how she felt, and of course she was for the South too, and I told her a little of what I was doing and she thought it was wonderful. "We going to have a separate country out here with Sacramento the capital and a whole passel of admirals and generals and ambassadors and ministers sashaying all around and horses and carriages and soldiers?"

"You got it all figured out."

"I been in a capital."

"Caracas?"

"Well?"

"For admirals you got to have a navy."

"In San Francisco Bay, isn't there enough room?"

"You're way ahead of me."

"And you, I bet you'll be President."

"Oh no, not me."

"You're the prettiest, why not?"

"You're the prettiest. What'll you be?"

". . . Don't you know?"

"Mrs. President."

But that didn't seem to go down at all, and she

kept asking me didn't I know what she'd be, and
seemed surprised I didn't know, and upset. She kept
staring out at the sun, where it was sinking into the
river, but when I mentioned we ought to take a
swim, she brightened up, and we took off our
clothes and went in. It was too cold to stay very
long, but we paddled around and splashed water on
each other, and her breasts drew up tight so she was
so slim you could hardly believe it. Then we dressed
and decided to eat supper back home. All the while
we were in the grove, the boats had been clunking
up and down, and the fishing sloops, and just as we
got our basket packed, here came a steam launch
going upriver and I hailed her and offered the Chi-
naman at the tiller a buck to tow us up to town and
he caught my painter and we sat back and took it
easy. It was pretty out there with the lights shining
over the water and the launch engine panting and
the Chink's face showing red every time he opened
his firebox and threw in a few chunks off his woodpile. A new moon was up there, but when I said
let's make a wish she began acting funny again and
curled up against my shoulder without saying anything.

Next day she was restless and didn't seem much interested when I said something about another picnic. We rowed upriver to the mud bar where my placer was, and she watched while I rocked out a spoonful of color, but then we rowed back and just sat around. After lunch she came back to where I was pumping up water into the shower tank and said she wanted to go out that night. "All right, if that's how you feel about it. But I warn you right now it's not the smartest thing you can do. They're looking for you, and those officers, they circulate. Soon as they win five dollars on a wheel, and lap up a couple of drinks on the house, they're off to the next place, and if we're circulating too, it's a hundred to one you'll be seen."

"Only one of them knows me."

"That deputy you vexed so? Isn't he enough?"

"I have a veil I can wear."

"You can't veil the shape, and unfortunately you uncovered so much of it for the captain that it's probably impressed on everybody's mind."

"Well, listen at him."

"That's something I don't forget in a hurry."

"The shape's on your mind too, then?"

28

"Looks a little that way."

"Then act like it."

She put her arms around me and I carried her inside, and after I acted like it a couple of times we lay there and she kept curling my hair around her finger and I said: "There's only one way it'll be safe for you to go over to Sacramento tonight and strut those places."

"What way is that?"

"If you're not wanted any more."

"I am wanted, though."

"Not if there's been some mistake."

She sat up on one elbow and looked at me a long time, her eyes with a shiny, fixed look to them like the eyes in a Chinese doll. "What do you mean by that?"

"I mean, you can never tell how things happen. If it was just a piece of foolishness, like you say it was, why maybe she's found her pocketbook by now. Or the one that took it has maybe got ashamed of themselves and sent it back. You never can tell about a thing like that. You could go over there. Row over and go down to the Wells, Fargo office and take one of their messengers and send him over to the Sheriff's office with a little note or whatever you want to send—and find out."

She kept staring, then laughed and kissed me. "Roger, you've given me the most wonderful idea."

Around four she rowed across and I lost sight of her behind a dray on the embarcadero. But after a while she was back, and after she tied the boat up she ran in the house and came out with the glass I used when a little looking had to be done. She sat down on the grass and began to watch. Two or three boats were at the piers, ready to pull out for the night run to San Francisco, and I thought she was watching the *Antelope,* that was tied up near the bridge. But the *Antelope* pulled out and she stayed where she was, and then I saw it was the bridge she was watching. Pretty soon a stagecoach clattered over, and she followed it with the glass. Then she let out a yelp like some child that got a rattle it wanted. "Oh, oh, oh! Just look at the old fool!" She handed me the glass, and sure enough, on top of the coach, riding with the driver and messenger, was the deputy. "Where's he going?"

"To grab me, in Cache Creek."

"How did he get that idea?"

"From a note, that was sent by Wells, Fargo."

By now, that money and the way they were looking for her were riding me plenty, but I couldn't
help laughing at the slick way she had cleared the
ground for a good time that night. The only people
in Sacramento that knew what she looked like were
the deputy and the woman. It didn't look like the
woman would be in the fast places, and that left
the deputy. But there he was, chasing his tail in
Yolo County dust.

I clipped out some stuff to mail, and when I went
in the bedroom it was a sight. She had taken her
dresses out and hung them up, to pick out which one
to wear. But how so many clothes could come out
of one small trunk was something you couldn't believe. There were red ones and blue ones and green
ones and silk ones with ruffles and satin ones with
nets to go over them. They caused me to go on one
or two more trips across the river before we started
out. One was to get a white shirt in place of the red
flannel ones I'd been wearing, like they had in '49,
and most of them haven't been washed since, if you

ask me. The other, once I got into the gray suit and topper I brought from Annapolis with me and hadn't even unpacked, was to get a cab. She decided on a black lace dress, with a great red flower pinned to the belt, and a little bonnet with ribbons, like a poke bonnet except it was all black lace, and I just couldn't bear fetching her there in a rowboat. The driver whistled when we pulled up at the shack, and she was something to see all right, as she came stepping out, holding up her skirt with both hands and looking so slim a breeze might blow her away. Talk stopped when we went in the Western for dinner, and all over the dining room you could hear them whispering about her and asking who she was. I tried to think about the money, but I couldn't, and all I could think of was how proud I was of her and how much I loved her.

We hit the gambling halls as soon as we put away some Hangtown fry and bear steak. She had a system gambling, and I never forgot it and it's made me plenty since. She'd stand at the roulette table as icy cold as something made of marble, and look at the wheel and yet not look at it, and never show any feeling at all, whether she was winning, losing, or just yawing along. She'd bet a buck on the first twelve, then as soon as she was playing on their money she'd up the bet to two dollars. Then when she got a little ahead she'd keep betting two dollars on the first twelve, but put one dollar on the first four. Then when she cashed her first double bet, she'd up the bet on the first twelve to five dollars, on the first four to two dollars, and lay a dollar bet on number one. That way, instead of coppering her bet, the way most of them do, she was lining it up for a killing when she really got one. The bets on the first twelve, when she cashed one, paid enough to keep her nearly even. But when she cashed on the first four, that was good odds, and she cashed on the first twelve too. And when she cashed number one, which she did a couple of times, it was real odds, plus good odds, plus some odds, and it wasn't long before she had a pile. It surprised me she could figure it up like that and didn't just trust to luck. Between those dresses and the silver that was stacked up so it touched her breasts, I began to see something I hadn't known was there.

I won a little too, and when I bought her a little

gold bracelet with a ruby in it, that was turned in by a woman having bad luck, she kissed it, and took me out in the street and kissed me, and when we went in the next place didn't gamble any more, but just stood by and watched me. One thing, though, seemed funny. Every place we went, we had hardly started to play before somebody would be alongside of her, whispering things in her ear, and three or four times I stepped in between and asked what they wanted. The last place, it was a slim, sunburned fellow with a little silky mustache. But when I stepped in between and asked him what he wanted, I was drawn to him like a breeching was behind me pulling me along, because he stepped back and something told me he had a gun and I had to keep close to him because my only chance was to hit him before he drew. The place stopped gambling like it had suddenly been froze, and he kept going backward and I stayed right with him, my belly almost touching his. But in one way I had the best of it. I could tell when he was going to bump the wall, and when he did I let him have it, right on the chin. He went down and I banged his head on the floor and felt his pockets.

When I had the gun I stuck it in my pocket and pitched a ten-dollar gold piece at the proprietor. "Will you have that mess cleaned up?"

"I'll attend to it, sir."

Back at the table she was looking at me with eyes as big as moon agates, but when I started to play again she hooked her hand in my arm and took me outside. She flagged another cab, and when we got in she kept holding tight on to my arm. When we were in the shack she took me in her arms and held me tight and began taking off my coat and hat and necktie. "I just love it you hit him for me."

"The dirty son of a bitch."

"I was so scared he'd shoot you."

"Me too, but I got him."

But later on, when it was just getting light, and I said I was going to give her a wedding ring a half inch wide so the bastards would know she was my wife and let her alone, she raised up and looked at me so long I knew it was the same old thing on her mind, whatever it was, that had set her off yesterday. And in the half dark her eyes always got so much bigger and blacker than they seemed in the daytime that it gave me a creepy feeling up my back, because I knew they said something I didn't understand. "Roger, you got no more idea than a June bug what I am, have you?"

"What do you mean, Morina?"

She burst out crying, and it was deep, ugly crying that shook her way down inside, so I knew that whatever it was about, it was terrible to her. I took her in my arms, but when I woke up she was gone, and so were her things and her trunk and my boat. It wasn't till three or four o'clock in the afternoon that a boy came rowing across with it, with a note. It said she had to leave and good-bye and she loved me.

I addressed my envelopes, put in my dispatches, and wrote Annapolis a note about the battalion of recruits that had started downriver that morning on a transport, bound for San Francisco. Then I rowed across, mailed my stuff, came back, and ate my supper. But when I brought a chair outside and sat down to wait till it was time to go to bed, I thought I'd die. Every boat that went clunking by reminded me of her, every frog in the tule patch made me pine for her. I tried to tell myself I was glad she was gone, that she was a thief, that she could only mean trouble and I ought to be dancing a hornpipe I was rid of her. It was no use. Around nine I put on my gray suit and white shirt again and rowed over to the city, looking for her. First I went to the restaurants, thinking she might still be at dinner. Then I went to the hotels. I didn't ask for her by name. I was afraid to, for fear they'd been notified to watch out for her, and it didn't look smart to, because she'd know better than to give herself away. I would go up to the desk, spin the register around, and start looking over the names, figuring I could spot her if she had come in that day. If they said anything, I told them I'd heard that a bunch had started out from my home town for the West, and I didn't know who they were, but could spot my friends if there were any. That looked harmless and I didn't have any trouble.

Then I went to the gambling halls, which was where I really expected to find her. I visited every roulette wheel, but what I found was nothing.

3

"*¡Ah! que bonitos
Son los enanos
Los chiquititos
Y mejicanos.*"

It was three nights later, and I'd looked until I
was sick of looking, and found there was kind of
a gang that went from one place to another, first
the bunch of army officers that were all over the
town, then the losers that wanted to change their
luck, then the girls that hooked a man and wanted
to take him some place else so nobody knew how
they got him, and then these here Mexicans that
play and sing and pass the hat for coppers. There
were two or three bunches, but the one with this
song had a leader named Paddy, that was short for

Padillo, and he was a bandy-legged little man with white teeth and a funny grin. He sang the song slow, so I could copy it in my notebook, and then I asked him: "But why do you stoop down when you sing this song?"

"Estoop? How estoop?"

"You don't call that standing up, do you?"

"No estoop—eshrivel! Thees song, is about liddle *enanos*—how you say—dwarfidos! Smalle pipple. So, sing song, make me small!"

He sang it again, and the other four joined in, and the song was pretty but the singing wasn't, which was why I wanted the words, so I could learn them and sing it to myself. So he kind of apologized for it: "Me, am really a miner. I sing in *mariachi* while my brodder, he get married, bring liddle *muchacha* wife from San Mateo."

"Well, I knew you weren't any singer."

That got a shout from the others, and after a while they said I should come up to their shack for supper, but not just yet, because they had quite a little to do before we could sit down to eat. So when the lights began to come on he and I strolled down to my boat and started upriver, but we hardly started out before somebody was calling him from a boat off the embarcadero. We pulled in, and the other four were there, and the idea was they were going to help themselves to a fish from a barge market that had live boxes alongside, in the river. The trouble was it was such a whopping big fish they couldn't handle it, and on account me being so big they thought I could do it. They took the top off a box and I stuck my hand in and maybe it was a fish but it felt more like a bear trap. I tried again, and again after that, and I was blood up to my elbow before I pulled it out, and it had hold of my thumb, and I saw it was an ocean crab as big around as a dinner plate. They quit laughing when I slung it at them, and a couple of them went overboard to get out of its way, but they hollered they knew I was no fisherman, and that evened it up for the guy about the singing, and from then on we were friends. Soon as Paddy got them quieted down so no wharf guards would get in it they used a bull's-eye lantern on another float and a big salmon practically jumped in the boat. I had eaten two pieces, and was all full of their tortillas and hot stuff, before I remembered this was stealing too, and if it was wrong for her, why was it just funny for me?

"Rodrigo."

"Yes, Paddy?"

We were lying in front of my shack, where he had rowed back with me to have a look at my rocker in the morning and maybe give me some tips, and I'd told him a little about Morina. Nothing about the money, or how I'd got her off the boat, but plenty about how she'd left me, and how I'd been looking for her. "Rodrigo, she no estay in Sacramento."

"How do you figure that out?"

"At estimbo, nobody meet, you say?"

"Not that I saw. She said her family's dead."

"And you no come, she meant estop in hotel?"

"That was the idea."

"She go to Nevada. I show you why."

We went in by the fire, and I got him pen, ink, and paper, and he drew a map of California, a better map than I could have drawn, a map that looked like something in a book. He put all the rivers in,

and showed how they lead up from the Golden
Gate, first the Sacramento, leading up to the mouth
of the San Joaquin, then bending around and leading up to the northern part of the state, then the
San Joaquin with twenty little feeder rivers, leading down to southern California, and showed how
the state would never need any railroads, with
steamboats to haul you any place you want to go,
and even the few railroads it has are starving to
death on account of no business. "Now, Rodrigo,
you listen. Here is a girl. If she want Stockton,
she take boat to Stockton. If she want Aliso, she
take boat to Aliso. Any place in California, she
take estimbo straight there. But she want Nevada,
first she estimbo San Francisco to Sacramento, then
she change to estimcar."

"What's she holding out on me?"

"Maybe her business roulette. Maybe she deal
faro, big Virginia City place, no want to tell you,
you think she is no nice girl. You go there, you
find."

"She's not here, that I'm certain."

"You go, write me, I come. Thees gold here, all
wash out."

42

That stuff he had figured out about the rivers and all wasn't new to me in any way, because I'd ridden the boats myself. Why I'd been shying off it was that I wasn't supposed to go to Nevada. I was supposed to stay in Sacramento and do my duty exactly the same as a soldier. I tried to tell myself it was not like being a soldier, that I ought to go to Nevada anyway, to see what was going on there. But all that got me was I woke up one night with the word *deserter* whispering in my ear.

You go by the cars to Folsom, and from there on over by stage, and I never saw such a road in my life. The way it's built, with grades and cuts and width and sprinkling carts wetting it down wherever it's a little dusty, you'd think it was built for Bragg's army. And from what was moving on it you'd think it was being used by Bragg's army, too. There was every kind of wagon you ever heard of, from prairie schooners to oxcarts to hayricks to Conestogas, besides an article I never saw until now, and even after you see it you're not sure you believe it. It's a Washoe wagon, that runs in three sections coupled together with three-foot tongues, all twelve wheels higher than a man's head, and the freight piled as high as a two-story house. They were run by different companies, each company with a different color, so of course the mules had tassels on their bridles the company's color, and when you saw twenty of them hustling a wagon along, all matched for color and size, all slicked up till you could see your face in their hide, all with harness oiled black and buckles polished yellow, all with sleigh bells jingling over their hames, and all with a muleteer in the saddle, cracking his whip and singing like hell, it was a sight. There were stagecoaches in a trot going uphill and a dead run going down, with drunks hollering inside and messengers outside taking potshots at bears. There were thousands of sheep, cattle, and pigs going on foot, and when they met mules it was war, but they gave what they got, I'll say that for them. There were hombres on horseback and occasionally one on foot, all headed for the Washoe country, all after those silver bricks they were digging out of Mount Davidson.

My coach was an Overland, and we'd stop at

one of the stables that ran for a mile outside of every town and change horses, then jog in to the hotel to pick up passengers and let them off. So I had two chances to get down and look around, specially at coaches going by on the road, to see if she might be in one. But all I saw was sports and drunks and women with paint on. I stopped for the night in Carson, made Virginia the next day, and put up at the International. Then I kept on like I had in Sacramento, looking in hotels, saloons, dance halls, and gambling places, every place I could think of.

In a bar that night a Union recruiting sergeant went up to a big, good-looking man at the bar and began to talk about signing him up. The man listened awhile and then he turned around and said: "How many times have you give me this spiel?"

"Three or four times, I guess."

"And how many times have I told you no?"

"Jack, there's a war going on."

"Then here's something that maybe you don't know: I'm paying for your goddam war, or at

least a big part of it, with this silver mine I've got,
and if you haven't been told about it, suppose you
stop by my office tomorrow and I'll show you a let-
ter from your own Secretary of the Treasury beg-
ging me to keep my output up and assuring me that
I'm doing more to help win this war right where I
am than I would be in command of five regiments."

"All right, Governor, now I know."

"That was when I volunteered."

"No need to get sore."

"Have a drink, and from now on let me alone."

I pricked up my ears at that, and next day when
I inquired around I found it was all true and
everybody in town seemed to know about it. The
silver from the Comstock Lode went down in a
steady stream to the mint in San Francisco, and
gold and paper came back. It wasn't just thousands,
it was millions and hundreds of millions. I knew I
had found out something then, something that
would make this trip all right, even to Annapolis.
I packed and caught the night stage for Carson, so
I'd lose no time getting back to my post and re-
porting about it.

Going out of Virginia, we passed the big omnibus

that ran between Virginia and Gold Hill, a place about a mile south, and out of the back door I saw the flutter of a skirt, black silk with white dots. I didn't ask my money back, or even wait. I had the driver stop, get out my carpetbag, and let me down. Then I ran after the omnibus, carrying my bag. At C and Union it stopped and she got out. I called, but she didn't hear me and turned the corner. When I got there I was just in time to see her turning into D, down the hill. I ran down, and saw her going into a house. I ran up to it, and had my hand on the bell to pull it before I noticed the light over the door. But then I knew why her eyes made me feel so funny.

It was red.

"You been to Biloxi's lately?"

"To hell with Biloxi. Her place stinks, her beer stinks, and she stinks. She's got no girls is her trouble. I'm sticking with the Twins. They take your money, but you get something for it. They've got the girls and they've got the sports, specially the big ones. What Biloxi's got is nothing."

"Maybe she's put in improvements."

"What kind of improvements?"

"That niece that got in this week."

"Any good?"

"You couldn't prove it by me. Biloxi's not dating her for anything I can afford. But there she is, just the same. And there's the stuff she brought with her, from San Francisco, Sacramento, and everywhere.

I'm telling you, Biloxi's getting ready to give the Twins some competition."

"What do you mean, stuff?"

"Mirrors, for one thing. Over every bed."

"*What?*"

"These women know something. They're from New Orleans."

It was a Saturday, in the International Bar, and I don't know how long I'd been sitting around there, but it must have been two or three days. I wanted to hit them both, but I was too sick to my stomach. I'd been hearing stuff like that everywhere, and I'd found out something I hadn't known before: a new girl in a house, it's all over town like a prairie fire, the biggest news of the week. But I couldn't have hit anybody for spreading it, because I'd have been ashamed to have them find out I even cared.

That night came the news of Chancellorsville, and from the glum way everybody took it I knew it was even better than it said in the paper. I tramped around, taking drinks, trying to feel good about it, but the liquor didn't take any effect, and after a while I knew where I was going. But when I turned into D Street I ran into something I'd never even heard of, all my life. It was what they call the Parade, about five thousand miners, cowmen, mule-skinners, mine-owners, sports, army officers, gamblers, bushwhackers, and just plain hombres with nothing to do, all shoving up one side of the street and down the other, beating on doors of houses, trying to get in. Most places had a little window, shaped like a diamond, in the front door, with a lace curtain over it, and now and then the curtain would be pulled to one side, and one, two, three, four, or five fingers would be held up, but mostly one finger, and then the riot would start. First, whoever was going had to be got out, and that took a minute of pushing and yelling and cussing. Then whoever was coming had to be got in, and that was worse, because everybody voted for theirself, so there was quite some difference of opinion. Then, finally, the door had to be shut, and that was worst of all, because arms and elbows and knees and feet were in the way, and then generally there were whiskers in the crack even after they got the key turned.

The number I wanted was 17, and when I got to it I beat on the door, but nothing happened. Then a little fellow in a Panama hat stepped up beside me and rapped with his stick, like it was a signal, but there was a terrific row going on inside, or an argument or something, and he didn't get any action either. So he turned to me and said: "You want in?"

"No, I'm just onry."

"Has to be this house? No other won't do?"

"I got a reason."

"There's eight or ten reasons in there, some of them pretty nice. I got one too, and if she knew I was outside I'd be inside pretty quick, but I'm just back from out of town and she's not any mind reader and there's too much noise going on in there for her to hear me knock. But there's one way. That is, if you're tall enough and you don't mind a ride."

"I'm six feet three."

"Then let's go."

We went to Union and turned uphill, and when we came to a hoisting works he unlocked the door and rolled it back. "Hold on, my young friend. Are you sure you know what you're doing, getting into that house by way of this mine?"

"Yes, I know."

"And the owner, he knows?"

"I'm the owner. I'm Jack Reiner."

" . . . How about that ride?"

"You'll see."

We went inside and he lit a lantern, and it was a great big room, two or three stories high, with a rectangular opening in the middle of the floor big enough to drop a ship in. It was the mine shaft, in four parts, with lifting cages at the top of three of them, and nothing at the top of the fourth except an iron rail to keep you from falling into the meanest hole I'd ever seen in my life. So of course that was our hole. And after we'd put on a couple of suits of overalls he took out of a closet, and put on miners hats with candles in them, and lit up, we started down a ladder that ran down beside a lot of pipes and stuff that he said were connections to the pumps. It was a rocky trip down, specially for one that had had as much to drink as I'd had, but after a while we reached a level place he called a station, and stepped off the ladder, and went in a tunnel that led off from the shaft. Then we stooped and squeezed until we got past a string of little mine cars that were standing there, and he told me to get in the front one—that is, the one futherest from the shaft. Then he lifted the coupling pin, kicked out the chock, and hopped in himself. First we rolled slow, but then we got up so much speed our candles went out. Then we went roaring through heat and steam and hot water dripping in our eyes and all of it pitch dark until I was scared so bad I didn't think I'd live till we hit, if we ever did. We did soon enough, when we fetched up against a bumper with a bang that almost knocked my teeth out. We did some more climbing, and then I saw where we were. The argument was still going on in 17, but we were behind it now, on the downhill side, and it was above us. On D Street, on the downhill side, the houses were all built on stilts, and hung out over the mines thirty or forty feet in the air. The lowest cross brace of 17 was three or four feet above my head, and I sat him on my shoulders and he caught it and went on up. I jumped and caught it with my finger tips, and skinned the cat some kind of way and got my knees over, and then after a little pushing and pulling we were both on the back porch, peeling off the overalls, which we hung on the rail. He laughed and said: "Hell of a lot of work for just a little fun, isn't it? Like the one they were telling at Donelson. The general and the major and the captain were arguing how much of it was work and how much fun, so they put it up to the private that was striking for them. He says: 'It's all fun. If there was any work attached to it, you'd have me doing it.' "

"Were you at Donelson?"

"With McClernand. Cold enough to freeze the ears off a brass monkey, too. I lost a toe. That's how I got my discharge."

"I had a brother with Buckner."

"You secesh?"

" . . . I might be. Why?"

"Biloxi'll love you."

"I haven't met her."

"Wait till she finds out."

She kissed me when Reiner told her, and then she really carried on. She was a dark, good-looking woman of forty, maybe not quite so old, with the same slim hips Morina had, big breasts pushed up high by her corsets, paint on her cheeks, and a funny way of talking that was half Gulf and half French. Her fellow was named Renny and he played the piano, and his friend was named Haines, and had a sweet tenor voice that made you cry. For me she had him sing *Dixie* and *Maryland, My Maryland*, and when a lieutenant hollered shut up with them goddam secesh pieces she grabbed up a sword with an ivory handle and engraving on it that had been made for a Mississippi general killed at Shiloh, stuck the point in his belly, and told him to get up and apologize. Then everybody laughed, and Reiner told him it was Biloxi's way and he might as well get up and apologize or get the hell out. So he said he'd be damned if he'd apologize but if she'd take the frogsticker away he would sing bass. So Renny started *Maryland, My Maryland* again, and he sang bass, and stead of secesh words it was German words he sang, but Biloxi was satisfied and put the sword away.

Then a fellow with a heavy gold watch chain that was sitting near the door said something to her, and she went to the foot of the stairs in the hall and started the same hollering we had heard from the outside. She kept calling Morina, and said Mr. Brewer was ready to bet and everybody was ready and to come on down and take their money from them. About the same time I placed Mr. Brewer he seemed to remember me, because he nodded and spoke. He was the one that had let the sergeant have it that night in the saloon, on whether he should enlist in the army or not. He leaned over and said he loved money all right but this was one bet he wanted to lose. I had begun feeling funny the minute I heard Morina's name, but I asked what the bet was, and he said never mind, but to get ten dollars down, because they weren't letting anybody look that didn't put up some dough, and I'd be hoping to lose too. About that time Morina came downstairs with a tall hombre and she was laughing at his jokes, whatever they were. She had on some kind of black silk wrapper, with red sash, red shoes, and a red ribbon in her hair. Biloxi kept hollering about the bet, and all the others joined in, but she said to hell with the bet, she was there for a good time and it was too much like work. She came in and sat down and told Haines to sing and he started the *Vacant Chair*.

56

Her seat was no more than three feet from mine, but he was in the second chorus and they had all joined in before she noticed me. And he had started something else, and they were all around the piano before she spoke. "What did you have to come here for?"

"Did I know you'd be here?"

"Of course you did!"

"How, for instance?"

"You followed me down! You called me!"

" . . . I came on business."

"I haven't got but one business."

Biloxi saw something was going on about that time, and came over and patted my hand and asked what it was, and tried to get something out of Morina, but she looked away toward the music and wouldn't talk. Then when Biloxi got it out of me I had wanted to marry Morina and had come down to talk it over, she put her arm around me and kissed me, and cried a little bit, and asked Morina why she treated me so bad. It kind of stabbed into my heart that Biloxi was on my side and, even if she was a madam in a house, wanted Morina to have a happy life and be with somebody that loved her.

All this time the music was going on, and the men and the girls were laughing and singing and carrying on, except Brewer would come over every couple of minutes and shake gold in his two cupped hands at Morina, but Biloxi would wave him off. And then pretty soon Morina turned to me and said: "Why do you tell her that? You know we can't ever be married."

"What's stopping us?"

"You're just a boy."

"I'm free, white, and twenty-one."

"You're nothing but a baby, and if I ever was crazy enough to marry you, you know just as well as I do you could never forgive me for what I've been. You'd hate me for it, and for every man that ever—"

"Went upstairs with you! Say it!"

I must have hollered that out, because all of a sudden there was no singing any more, and they were all looking at me, and Biloxi was looking at me, with kind of a little smile twitching around her mouth. "My *petit Annapolitain* play little bit? Until he grow up? Fall in love, yes? Have fun?"

"I guess that's got to be it."

It was a minute before Morina looked at me, and then I said: "You heard what she said. So all right. So what's the price of doing business?"

She didn't cry, but her eyes began to glitter like they were made of glass. "Why did you have to say that, Roger? Couldn't you let Biloxi have a sweet feeling about you? Couldn't you let me keep the three days I spent with you, and the love I feel for you? Why do you have to mess it all up?"

"I asked you your price."

"To you, one thousand dollars."

"You'll get it."

I told her there was nothing she wouldn't be, from a thief to a whore, for a thousand dollars, and that's how I knew I'd get her for it, and that's why I'd be back. Biloxi asked me to go. I said how she'd like to try putting me out, and she got up and walked over to the sword, and I was hoping she'd try to use it, because I wanted to hit her, and Morina, and wreck her place. But all of a sudden Morina jumped up and waved her back and turned to me. "So you think you want to stay?" And when I still sat there, she went over to Brewer. "How much you want to bet?"

59

"Anything you say."

"I'll cover a hundred."

"I cover five!"

Biloxi screamed it, and next off, she was covering gold that everybody was slapping down on the piano, until a pile was there that must have been seven or eight hundred dollars. Then Morina picked up a beer bottle, emptied the beer out the window, and climbed on top of the piano. "Roger, I've bet this gentleman here I can do something he's never seen done, something he thinks can't be done, something nobody thinks can be done. But we don't have deadheads looking at me. If you want to stay, put up some money. If you're not going to bet, now is the time to get out."

She whipped off the wrapper and a fellow whistled. Except for the ribbon in her hair and the red shoes on her feet, she didn't have a stitch on, and she never looked more beautiful or more horrible. *"Are you going to bet?"*

She kicked, and a slipper hit me in the face. I held on for another second, and then I ran. I ran out back, the way I came in, and I just made the rail in time. It seemed a year before all the stuff I had drunk splashed down below, and before it did, a yell went up inside. I went down the scantlings ashamed and licked and scared. I ran till I came to a street, but when I came to a saloon I went in. If it killed me, I had to have a drink.

Around three o'clock I was at the International, sitting around the bar, afraid to go to bed for fear of what I'd think about when the light was out and it was dark. An officer came in and ordered rye. He raised his glass at me and I saw it was the young lieutenant that had got into the row with Biloxi over the song. "You left too soon."

"I had to run. I was sick."

"It's all you can hear down there—the hundred she made out of it, the five she made for Biloxi, and the extra change she made for the girls. It's all over the street. They say it'll put Biloxi's place right on top. They say it'll even put her in front of the Twins."

"Pretty slick."

"Brewer, he loved it."

"He can have her."

61

"He did."

Things began to go round, and he said a lot, but I didn't hear what it was. Then he was asking me something: "You know what she did?"

"I don't much care."

"She—"

"I said I don't care what she did."

"She stood on one foot, and —"

"You want to take a dive in that spittoon?"

"Well, if that's how you feel about it."

"That's how I feel about it."

I never did find out what she did. What was coming out of their throats when they were yelling in there was all I wanted to know about it. They sounded like a pack of hyenas.

> *"Sale la linda*
> *Sale la fea,*
> *Sale el enano*
> *Con zo zalea."*

It was him all right, plunking the same guitar, singing the same song, eshriveled in the same foolish way. I ran over there fast, because I think I was gladder to see him than I had ever been to see anybody in my life. I had moved out of the International by now, because my money was running low, to a boarding house on B Street, and my shoes were wearing out and my hat was caving in, and still I couldn't get up enough gump to get a job or leave the place or do anything but hang around the saloons and pretend what I was going to do when I got me a thousand dollars, and after that I was going to get the hell out. I had seen her once or twice, with this or that big sport, but mostly with Brewer, and she was carrying every inch of silk, satin, and lace that her sticks would hold.

But when I went running over to him, where he was on the boardwalk with some other Mexicans, he just gave me a quick handshake and motioned me to wait, and went on singing till he had a crowd. Then he began making a speech, in Spanish. What it was about I couldn't understand, but they all followed him close, and nodded at each other, and whispered. It wasn't till he had written down some names and appointed some kind of a committee that he let his meeting break up. Then he took me to a little Spanish place on Silver Street, and only when we were sitting down to a table and he had ordered some red wine did he really shake hands and show his white teeth and look me over and ask me how I'd been. I said all right, and asked for his brother and the other boys in Sacramento, and he said the little *muchacha* was dancing with the *mariachi* now, and they were doing so well they had a job riding a steamboat. Then, like he didn't remember at all what I'd come here for, he said: "And you, Rodrigo? You marry, yes?"

"Not yet, Paddy."

"Some day, with nice *muchacha*."

" . . . I found her."

"Thees Morina?"

"Just like you said."

I told him, then, something about it, not much, because talking about it upset the hell out of me, but a little bit. He shook his head, and after a while said: "In Mexico, not so bad. In Mexico, each do own work, and if liddle *muchacha* do thees work, take care of mamma maybe, give papa fine serape, what more can liddle *muchacha* do? Fallow love her, pay not attention. In thees country, is not so good."

"It stinks in any country."

"M'm—so."

"Would *you* like it?"

"Rodrigo, I like you."

I knew, of course, he was only trying to soften it up a little, so it wouldn't hurt so bad, so I shut up and we sat there awhile, not saying anything. Then: "What you do here, Rodrigo?"

"Kill flies for the bartenders."

"But you work, yes?"

"I got work waiting for me in Sacramento."

"Thees rocker? Pah!"

"There's some other stuff, too."

I had never told him about what I was doing for Annapolis, and for some reason didn't want to. If I did, I had to admit some stuff that was heavy on my heart, but if he didn't know it, at least there was that much he wouldn't look down on me for. I could feel him studying me, and he must have figured there was some lying to it somewhere, because he said: "Rodrigo, how you like to come work with me?"

"In a mine? Would be pretty tough for me."

"Is only part."

"And what's the rest of it?"

"You hear me tonight? Make spich Mexican miner, on a corner, after liddle plinka-plank and liddle song? I start a union. Right here in Virginia City, I get thees men together, thees Mexican fallow, in miners' union."

"You mean a loafing association."

"That is what is called."

"That's what it is."

"Rodrigo, I work in mine all over Estados Unidos, all over Mexico, see many mine, many town. Never, in my whole life, do I see such 'orrible mine, such throw away man's life only to make money, such rich man no give a good goddam if poor man live or die, as here in thees place, Virginia City. Yes, one time I think like you, union is loafing association. But now I know, must come. Thees bad man, they no do for miner, then miner must say, yes you do. I make you."

"Quite a speech you got."

"To Mexican, yes. For American, I need you."

"Sorry, it doesn't interest me."

"Rodrigo, you need. To forget thees girl."

"I'm all against unions."

"You make big mistake."

I was almost asleep that night when it came to me, like a big bell ringing in the dark: with a union, if I could start it and run it and stop it when I chose, I could close down Virginia City tighter than the lid of hell, and stop that river of silver that was running east and furnishing the money to the North that they needed to win the war. I lay there

67

so excited I couldn't sleep, because that would make
it all right about my being here, and I could write
Annapolis, and my leaving Sacramento wouldn't
be something I had to be ashamed of any more.
I waited as long as I could, but it was still dark
when I ran down C Street and over to Gold Canyon,
where he and two or three friends had their shacks.
He was frying his beans when I got there, and
showed his teeth and laughed when I told him about
changing my mind, even if he had no idea what
my reasons were. He took me over to the Dakota
then, which was the mine he worked in, to get a
job, because of course I couldn't organize any
union unless I had a job in the mines. We lined up
in front of the timekeeper's window, outside the
stockade, us and the twenty or thirty that wanted
jobs that day, and after a while Trapp came out,
the foreman that needed men.

He was a big, heavy-set man, and there was a lot
of talk about him as he went down the line, feeling muscles and looking at hands and feet and
teeth, like we were a bunch of mules at a stock
auction. He came from Ohio, one man said, but

had been a slave dealer in Memphis up to 1858, when he did things that were too much even for that place, and when a couple of mulatto girls died in his barracks he got run out and came west. Even the mine-owners couldn't stand him, and he kept getting fired, but could always get a new job because though he treated the miners bad he could get out the ore, and there was generally somebody that needed him. He picked about a dozen of us and took us inside, and the timekeeper fixed us up with overalls, tools, hat, and candles, and booked us with them, around fifty dollars, and then we were brought in to the owner and the super-intendent. The owner was named Hale, and he was a little man around fifty with a pale skin, black mustache, and expensive clothes, that looked like a dignified rat. The super was a big rawboned man named Lew Williams that was dressed in cor-duroys and talked with a brogue. He made us a speech and said he came up from the face of the rock himself, back in Cardiff, Wales, and asked nothing from a man but good work, in return for which he expected to give him fair treament. Then he shook hands all around, but when he came to me asked my name. "And what part of the world do you come from, Duval?"

"Annapolis, Md."

"And what did you do there?"

"Went to college, mostly."

"Ah, the naval school?"

"No. There's a college there too, St. John's."

"And you took the diploma?"

"Yes sir. A.B."

"But you worked as well as studied?"

"I was a page for the legislature a couple of sessions. Then, when I was in college, I worked a bugeye three summers."

"A bug—?"

"It's a boat. Pointed at both ends, raked masts, leg-o'-mutton rig, centerboard. Really, it's an over-size, decked-over canoe. In the ocean they'd slide all around, but in the bay, with the board coming up for the sandbars, they handle all right. The oyster-men use them, and my boat I rented to naval officers when they felt like a sail down the bay for some fishing. They said it was fishing. From where

70

I stayed, at the tiller, it sounded more like poker-playing."

"And whisky-drinking, no doubt."

"Plenty of that."

"What's your weight, my lad?"

"One eighty, sir."

"Drop in and see me, Duval."

Going to the cage, the rest of them had plenty to say about teacher's pet and the boy on the burning deck, but Paddy shook my arm and I let them get away with it.

They tell you Virginia was laid out for hell but the devil's health couldn't stand it, and it's easy to believe once you've been there. It's on the side of a big mountain with a flag on top of it, called Mount Davidson. Half the streets run almost straight up and down, and they have names. The other half, they run level but they're tilted on one side, and they have letters. All over the place dust rises from the stamping mills that break up the ore, and in between the dust are big clouds of brown,

yellow, and green chemicals they use to amalga-
mate the silver, depending on which formula
they're using, and practically every mill has a different one, because the process peddlers are in
every saloon, and they've got everything from sul-
phuric acid to cyanide. The houses are made of
everything there is, brick or shingle or frame or
tin or sheet iron, but not one has a tree or flower
or blade of grass near it, or even some moss in
the chinks of the front walk. Some of the stores
are big, three or four stories high and covering
a whole block, but they're ugly and you have to
push and shove to get to a counter. The mines,
they're everywhere, with fences around them and
signs that say Keep Out and guards walking up
and down, and back of every mine is a tailings
dump, and to one side is a pile of busted cars and
rails and machinery. Practically any time you look
on C Street, which is where the big stores and offices
are, is a traffic jam, with coaches and wagons and
cattle and pigs all snarled up together, and the
muleteers shooting dice while the peace officers
straighten it out, and the cussing and whip-crack-
ing and mooing and hee-hawing are so loud you

can hear it a mile. The hee-hawing they've got a name for. They call it the soft warble of the Washoe canary, meaning a jackass. The Washoe part I didn't get straight for a while, but it's the name of some mountains up the line a little way, and some Indians too, and some people use it for all of that end of Nevada, so that's why they holler Washoe and mean anything from the town to the silver bricks to the mountains to the Indians to the state, or maybe nothing but they're drunk and feeling a little high. Then everywhere you look are Chinamen, that work all around and jam the streets. Then, down Six-Mile Canyon they've got a cemetery, but it's a hell of a civic problem, because what with sudden death from lead poisoning in the saloons, and smallpox and mine fires and falling cages and one thing and another, they can't ever get the cemetery big enough. The undertaker parlors, they're always complaining, but I never could see why, because even if they didn't do anything but rent out their tin flowers they still would be getting along all right. The tin flowers are in place of real ones that don't grow so well in Virginia, and after the funeral they collect them and use them on the

73

next fellow—that is, if they got time to rush them
around to the next fellow's residence, because they
fall fast, and sometimes the funerals conflict.

I had seen all that stuff, but I didn't know the
hundredth part of what they meant by the devil and
his health till I dropped down in the cage that morning to the thousand-foot level and saw what men
would do for four dollars a day. That steam that
comes out of the shafts and scares you to death
comes from boiling springs down under, and those
boiling springs are what the miners have all around
them while they get out the ore. Practically every
tunnel has hot water running between the rails, under the square sets, to the shaft, and at the bottom of
that is a sump, and into the sump runs the suction
ends of the pipes that run to the pumps. It didn't
take me any week to hate Hale, or any other owner
that would let men work in a place like that, or
Trapp, who stood over us like some overseer on a
cotton plantation, and had men dragged out by the
heels when they fainted in the heat, and set me to
throwing water on them, because I was new at the
work and there wasn't much else I was good for
until I learned my way around. By the time Paddy

took me to a crosscut where it was cooler, and we had our first jackbite, I was willing to pitch powder into the place and light it, I was so sore. Paddy said what we needed was blowers, but they'd require a bigger boiler and more transmission belts, and Hale was too cheap to put them in.

At night we held street meetings, but right away we hit a snag: we had to find some way to get Americans to listen to it, because they wouldn't stop for Paddy and his guitar. After a while he remembered a fellow named Newt, that loaded ore on weekdays but on Sundays he played the cornet in church. We looked him up, and if you ask me he thought the union was some kind of a fraternal organization like the Odd Fellows, but on an offer to play his cornet, all he could say was yes. So that night he came with us and played *Listen to the Mocking Bird* with curlicue variations, but Paddy could chord along on the guitar, and the miners stopped to listen and I began handing it out. I asked them how much longer they were going to stand for it, to be treated like so many mules on a picket line. I asked them did they think the owners were going to do something for them just from love, or because somebody made them do it. I asked them did they like to get burned up in fires, or were they going to organize and compel the owners to put in the things that would make the mines safe. I asked them plenty, and I had never made any speeches, but I was surprised to find I was pretty good at it. Sometimes they would grunt at you like they thought you had it figured out right, and sometimes they'd cut in on you with mean questions. But even then you knew they were interested in what you said.

After the street meetings we'd go in the mines. Those that were in bonanza worked three shifts, and Paddy knew every drift and shaft, and how to get in and how to get out. Around jackbite time we'd slip into the Savage or the Sierra Nevada or the Kentuck, and the men would hear the guitar and slip in a dead entry or wherever we were, and we'd douse the lights and for twenty minutes I'd shoot it. They didn't cut in on me then. Time meant too much and the steam was too near. It was coming our way, you could see that, so pretty soon we came

down to brass tacks. We set a date for a meeting, a
real one, with every miner in town expected to attend, on Sunday night, when they'd be free. We
appointed captains and committees and wrote down
names and really worked. And at the Dakota, from
the way Trapp acted and Hale acted and Williams
acted, you could see they were worried. One night,
as I was coming out, the timekeeper said Williams
wanted to see me. I went in there, and he looked me
over close and asked me to sit down. "Duval, you're
one of the leading spirits in this union, is that
right, my boy?"

"I don't say I'm not."

"You could be *the* leading spirit."

"We got plenty of leading spirits."

"Not like you. I attended your boardwalk meeting last night. You didn't see me, but I was there.
You seem to have a talent for gab, my boy."

"If I have, you gave it to me. You and Hale."

"How so?"

"By giving me plenty to gab about."

"And quite a wit you have too. Now, let's be
frank, what are your complaints with this com-

pany? You seem to be a reasonable young fellow, intelligent, educated, well-born—what's the real reason for this thing you're doing?"

"The whole system's wrong."

"Nothing personal?"

"Like what?"

"Ah—Trapp, for instance."

"He's a dirty, cruel, son of a bitch."

"If that difficulty were adjusted, would that take care of whatever you expect to deal with by means of a union?"

"It would help, but we'd still organize."

He studied me, and I expected him to lash out with something hot, and fire me, but he didn't. He nodded and said he just wanted to get straightened out, and when I told Paddy, he was proud I had handed it back just as good as I got, and told the other Mexicans, and we had a little celebration, with vino, before we slipped in the mines for our night's work.

Saturday before the big meeting, at lunch time, I called our gang together in the Dakota. It kind of

78

choked me up a little, the way they looked to me to
tell them the way it was to be done, and I looked
them all in the eye before I began to talk. There
were Lee and Cam, the two colored strikers, that
were wizards at sinking a drill with six-pound
hammers; Olesen, a big blond Swede, one of the
strongest men I ever saw; Hook, a one-armed fellow that got his hand mashed off when he was a
hand on a boat in the Erie Canal, and has a hook
in its place; Gator, a fellow from Cairo, that claims
he used to be an alligator man on a flatboat, and
Ronnie, a sixteen-year-old boy. I made it quick,
when I did begin to talk, and said the main thing
was to get the men there, we'd do the rest after the
meeting started. Paddy, he made a little speech too,
then Ronnie got up and started to say something,
some kid speech that didn't mean much, but when
Gator tried to shut him up everybody hollered to
let him talk.

It was just about that time that something jumped
out from behind the water barrel, and before we
could even move, Trapp was in the middle of the
entry, laying right and left with a tamping iron,
and he'd got a couple of them on the head in the

first couple of swipes. All the time he was swinging he was screaming: "Get out of here! Get back to work, you yellow-bellied rats! I know what you're doing! I heard every word that was said!"

With that I reached him, and he began swinging at me. "And you, Duval, the ringleader! You think you'll ever work again in this town? You needn't even stop for your time! You're fired without pay, and—"

"You'll pay me or you'll wish you had!"

"Out! Out of here! Or I'll—"

He'd been swinging with the tamping iron, but I'd been too close to him for him to hit me solid. He jumped back now, drew the iron back like it was a rifle with a bayonet, and tightened up to drive it. I caught his chin with everything I had, and when he went down I jumped on him and banged his head up and down on the rail and smashed my fist down on his face, then got up and kicked him. But in a minute it made me sick and I stood there blowing. Then I looked around and I was the only one except Trapp in the entry. The candles were all there, where we had stuck them on the timber to give us plenty of light, but not one man. In a minute the picking started, away over in the crosscut, and lights began to flicker, and the sound of rock hitting mine cars. They had run out on me.

But the word had gone out somehow, because down the entry a light showed, and by its wobble I knew it was the super. He came and looked at Trapp, then for a minute at me, and then he called the men. His voice sounded like the crack of a muleteer's whip. "Who did that?"

". . . I did."

I didn't answer him till he asked it two or three times and they had a chance to say something if they were going to. "Just you?"

"That's right."

"You didn't have any help?"

"No, I didn't."

"And what for?"

"You want to find that out suppose you begin cussing me out and treating me worse than a dog the way he did."

"You mean that?"

"You heard me."

"All right. Take charge."

". . . What?"

"I said, take charge and begin loading ore. Men, Duval's foreman from now on. Get this man washed up, put him on a car, and send him to the shaft, where I'll have him taken up in the cage. Well, Duval?"

"Yes sir. I'll do my best."

They sluiced off Trapp, and rolled him to the shaft on a car and came back, and started for the face of the rock. Then Ronnie came back to me. "Are you taking that job, Roger?"

"Mr. Duval."

"And how about the union?"

"I'm holding a company job, now."

"You two-faced son of a bitch."

"Ronnie, you're fired. Get out, and quick."

Paddy tried to tell them it was something any man ought to feel free to do, take a company job if they offered it to him. But they hated me for it, and they didn't hate me any more than I hated myself. Because Paddy could talk all he pleased, but if I didn't owe the men, I owed my country, or what

I called my country, to stick with something that might help it win. But when I heard the word *foreman,* my head began to pound with the thought of the thousand dollars it would give me, and what I meant to do with it.

6

They held their meeting, and instead of me for president they elected a fellow named Ferguson, and then they held some more meetings, and rumors began going around about what they were going to do, but they didn't call any strike because it turned out they didn't have to. The territory was to be a state soon, with an election for everything with a salary attached to it, and the politicians were so hot for votes they began putting the squeeze on the owners to treat the miners right. So everywhere you heard talk about blowers and fire buckets and even a tunnel from the mouth of Six-Mile Canyon to drive under the mountain and drain the hot water into the canyon mouth. But in my mine the men had nothing to say, and while they did like I told them, they didn't look at me, they didn't say good morn-ing and they didn't say good night. And then some things happened. One day a mine car came rolling down an entry and almost mashed me against the rib. Another day a timber crashed down from the top ledge of a stope and missed me about three inches. Another day I went flat on my face from a shot, but nobody had warned me it was lit.

And then one night I ran into her. It was the Sunday night after I drew my first time as foreman, $120 for two weeks at ten dollars a day. I had just finished dinner at the International, roast beef, potatoes and gravy, stewed peaches and coffee, and I had poured myself a second cup when she came in with Brewer. I had heard about what he was buying her, the pony cart, rings, clothes, and hats, but I wasn't quite prepared for what she looked like in all that stuff. The dress was crimson silk, with a big floppy lace hat, and yellow flowers pinned to one shoulder. Her face was all painted up, and she had lace gloves on with the fingers cut off so they stuck through bare, and on every finger were at least six rings with diamonds. She looked exactly like what she was. Brewer took her to a big table in

85

the middle, and then here came Biloxi all dressed up too, and Renny in evening clothes with a white tie, and Haines dressed even fancier than Renny. I drank my coffee and paid my bill, and I didn't hurry that I know of, but just the same, when I was done I left.

I got down to C Street, and could feel my face burning, and turned into a place and took a seat and ordered a glass of beer and watched them gamble. About six of them were near me, playing roulette and losing their shirt, three or four men and a couple of girls, and all of a sudden I thought about her system and the money in my pocket and stepped over and laid down a silver dollar. I laid it on the first twelve and lost. I followed it with the same bet on the same twelve and won. I was a buck ahead. I let it lay and won again. I was three bucks ahead and I laid one on number one, one on the first four, and one on the first twelve. The ball dropped in three, and I was ten bucks more to the good. I kept it up, and soon as the croupier took an interest and the others began to follow my lead, I quit. Because with them all over the board he'd have a hard time staking me out, because if he

didn't have to pay me he'd have to pay them. But
with all of them aboard the same numbers, his play
was so easy he wouldn't have been human if he
didn't make it.

But I had $45 of his money, and I drifted on to
the next place. I won $300 there and next door, and
across the street, and began to realize I was riding
a run of luck, as well as playing one hell of a system. And I had this excited feeling it wasn't going
to let me down. I won and lost here and there, and
my winnings kept rising, and then pretty soon I
upped the ante and left ten dollars on number one,
with ten dollars on the first four and another ten
dollars on the first twelve, as usual. And the ball
dropped in number one. I cashed $450 in gold, and
went back in the washroom to count up. With what
I'd been paid and what I'd won, I had $1,085.

Back in the hotel, Renny was at the piano, and
Haines was facing the people, getting ready to sing.
Renny was tall and thin and dark, with an olive
tint to his skin and kinky black hair. He was around
thirty, and Creole French. Haines was an Irishman,

kind of stocky, with a round, good-looking face,
China-blue eyes, and sorrel gold hair. When I got
in there, he was making a little speech, saying he
didn't often get a chance to sing for such a distin-
guished audience in Virginia City, but so long as
he was here he was going to sing some arias he had
used in a tour he made with an opera company in
Italy or France or Germany or wherever the hell it
was they took the show out. So that got a big hand,
especially from some women over in one corner
that seemed to be from out of town. So that was the
first I heard of Italian opera, which he sang in
Italian and Renny played without notes or anything. I found out afterward that opera was what
he and Renny lived for, only of course they never
bothered with music like that on a big Saturday
night at Biloxi's.

I didn't break in on the singing at all. I just took
a seat in the bar and listened to the music, and kept
an eye on things so nobody walked out or anything
before I got around to what I was there for. Then
after five or six selections, when Haines had got a
big hand and he and Renny had sat down to the table
again, I went in and walked over and clicked my heels

in front of Morina. "Good evening, Miss Crockett."

". . . Roger, what do you want?"

"An engagement, whenever you're free."

"What do you mean, engagement?"

"Business."

"I told you once, no."

"That's not what you told me. It's what you would have told me if you didn't love money more than you love anything else on earth. What you told me was, for one thousand dollars business would be done. All right, I've got the one thousand dollars, and I want to make a date."

Her eyes flickered, and while it soaked in I spoke to the others. None of the men said anything. Brewer lit a cigar and looked at me under the heavy black eyebrows that he had. Renny had eyes like a snake, and kept them on me without winking or showing expression of any kind. Haines kept looking at Brewer, wondering why he didn't do something, and not knowing what Brewer must have known, which was what happened to Trapp when he did something. But Biloxi put out her hand, and smiled, and pulled me down for a little kiss. "My little *Annapolitain* is back, 'allo Rogay! Come, let me ask something. Why you no let my Rina alone, ha?"

"Just want her, that's all."

"But I 'ave ozzer girl. Prettier girl."

"That's impossible."

"You come down, I show you. Li'l girl, 'alf Irish, 'alf *Chinois*, oh, oh, oh! Such 'air, such skin, such eyes! Is fourteen, jost right for my *petit Annapolitain*!"

"She sounds good, but first—"

"Roger."

"Yes, Morina."

"I'll see you in a few minutes."

"I'll be waiting for you, over there in the bar."

I went back to the bar, and next time Haines got up to sing, she came in there. "Roger, this has to end. You have no right to follow me around the way you do, and—"

"*I?* Follow *you?*"

"I can't stir out of the house that you're not there, watching me, counting how much money I bet, how much I win, how much I lose, what I have on, who I'm with—"

"Can I help it if I happen to be there?"

"It don't just happen."

"Have it your way."

"Roger, you asked me something just now. I don't want anything of the kind. I'd hate it. But if it makes you happy, if you're willing to have that and leave, you can go on down to the house and I'll be with you directly."

"What do you mean, leave?"

"Get out of Virginia City, go back where you came from, do what you're supposed to do, the wonderful things you told me about, the first night we were together, forget me and this place and everything else you're not in any way fit for."

". . . All right then."

"You'll be a lot happier."

"What about this other hombre? This Brewer?"

"That's none of your business."

She stepped in the lobby, snapped her fingers for a boy, told him to get her carriage. I paid for my drinks and started on down.

I had just crossed C, taking the short steps you always took to keep from sliding down the hill, when I heard the footsteps behind me. They came in a rush, like somebody rolling a drum, and then all of a sudden I was hitting and kicking with everything I had, and getting it through my head, too late, that what I had really done, with that trip through the roulette wheels, was collect a gang at my heels, and a gang that was out to get me, first chance it got, on account of what I'd done to the union. I'll fight anybody if I have to, but nobody's good enough to fight ten, or twenty, or however many there were. I went down, and they began kicking and stomping and spitting. A kick missed me, and caught my coat pocket, and gold coins spilled over the street in a shower, and went bouncing and rolling down the hill, even past D Street. They left me and ran after the money, yelling like Indians and fighting each other about it. A deputy rounded the corner at C Street and drew his gun and still they kept on hollering and fighting and picking up gold. He helped me up and asked what had happened. I told him nothing, and as soon as he left me and started toward the ruckus, I slipped away. Because in front of the hotel I could see her and Biloxi getting into a pony trap, and I didn't any more have the thousand dollars.

7

After I woke up a few nights, hearing those feet come at me from behind, I got out the .36 I took from the fellow in Sacramento. But I wouldn't have kept it if it hadn't been for the fellow in Scholl & Roberts where I went to exchange it for a .44, and get me some caps and paper cartridges. He listened, then asked me what I expected to shoot. "Nobody, if I can help it. Otherwise, anybody looking for trouble."

"But not no elephants?"

"They got elephants here?"

"Not that I know of."

"Then why do you ask?"

"Mister, my job is to sell guns, and if you want a .44 I've got a .44. But short of a elephant, I'd like you to tell me something a .44 will kill that a .36 won't, and do it better."

"Dead is dead. What's better?"

"Better is quicker."

"You take this awful serious."

"Don't you?"

I kind of shut up then and let him talk: "There's four main points to shooting, and only four: the draw, the aim, the fire, and the recoil. But they're all important, equally important."

"I begin to get the idea there's no unimportant points."

"That is correct, but you'd be surprised how many unimportant things men get their minds on, like how pretty they look, how much noise they make, how loud their artillery entitles them to talk —all good points on Sunday morning in church, where they got the Ten Commandments. But on Sunday night in the saloon, where all they got is the Golden Rule, do unto others as they would do to you, only do it first, only important things are going to do you any good. First now, consider the draw. A .44, you've got to carry it on a belt holster, no matter whether you sling it on your right hip, your

94

left hip, or across your belly. You've got to strap that holster end to one leg, and its uncomfortable, and there's always the chance that when you draw, that was when you had the thing hitched around a bit, to ease it, and the gun jams with unfortunate, not to say fatal, consequences. The .36 fits comfortable into an armpit holster, the only way to carry arms, and specially this .36 does. That's a navy gun, my friend, made in the Colt London factory; if you look at the engraving on that cylinder, you'll see it's a battle at sea. And it's one of the few models that were made with a short barrel, so it really does tuck under your arm there nice and snug and inconspicuous. Try it there. See how natural it is for your hand to go to it? Just like going to your heart. Your arm coddles the holster, so there's no sticking, fouling, or jamming. And when it comes out, it's about two feet closer to the line of vision than a gun coming out of a belt holster and that's a fraction of a second saved, but it could be the difference between yes and no or, as we say, perpendicular or planted."

"Did you learn all this by heart?"

"And I hope you will."

"The aim comes next."

"On that point there's also a great deal of un-
reliable stuff told. You'll hear about hip and fan
shooting, and undoubtedly there's been some, with
monuments commemorating the results. But I'm
telling you there wasn't any proper cause and
effect. It was simply accident, or you could say
luck. There's only one way to aim a gun. Bring the
sights in line with the target and your eye. Do it as
quick as you can, but do it, or you're liable to wish
you had. Noting once more that you can level a
nice handy gun like this one quicker than a big
one, I pass to the subject of fire. Here the same
principle is still guiding us. A .44 is simply too
big. Even if you aim it, by the time the heavy
trigger pull is taken into consideration, you've
twitched your weapon out of line, and accurate
shooting is impossible. Naturally any gun, no
matter what caliber, needs some work to bring the
trigger pull to where it's exactly right for you. I
don't mean hair trigger, you understand. A hair
trigger is nothing but a fool's way to get his thumb
shot off, or whatever shot off that happened to be
in the way, and with a belt holster it might not be

his thumb. But get a whetstone and stone your notch, so the gun is as much a part of you as your hand is. And even on that point the lighter gun is better. And now I come to the point so seldom thought of, the lack of whose proper appreciation has had so many, many sad but final consequences. A .44, I don't care if you've got the arm of a grizzly bear, is simply going to yank your hand up three feet in the air, and you're not going to shoot it again, to hit anything, until you've pulled it down, aimed it, and fired it. But a .36—"

"Is this holster for sale?"

"It is, but I've got a better one."

"It sounds expensive."

"It is, but you'll thank me."

It was a beauty all right, all hand-stitched in limp, tanned buckskin, with straps to hold it in place and a set to it that fitted the gun under your coat so most people would hardly notice it. I took it, and some ammunition, and thanked him for his lesson, and next night, around sundown, sneaked down Six-Mile Canyon to a gully where there was nobody around, stuck a playing card up on the timbers of an old drift, and went to work. Every.

thing he told me, I found out, was true, and specially what a fine gun I was using. I bought a stone
and took it down, and worked on spring and hammer and pins and everything else in there, and
wiped everything with machine oil and dried it, so
every night it was better and then one night it was
right. And then came the night when I could shoot.
At ten feet I'd put up a six spot of hearts and knock
holes in the spots as fast as I could pull the trigger.
At fifteen feet I could hit three but stay on the card,
and at twenty I could hit the card. I taught myself
to keep shooting whether I hit the target or not. Because another important thing, I figured, was to
get the habit of doing it a certain way, because
when the time came, if your hand didn't do it before your head woke up, why probably it wouldn't
wake up.

My real practice came by accident, one night
when I was ready to go home. I heard something
behind me, and before I knew it I had wheeled and
fired and a jack rabbit went straight up in the air
and when he lit he was dead. Then I noticed the
moon coming up, and all around rabbits were
coming out and starting to play. I stayed there and

practiced what I needed most, which was to wheel and shoot at anything coming from behind. I brought so many rabbits home to Mrs. Finn, who ran the boarding house I lived in, that the other boarders began to complain. A jackass rabbit is not like a cottontail. He's long, lean, and tough.

All that time I saw a lot of Paddy, because even if he wished I hadn't cut the union, we were friends and took walks and talked. Then one Sunday he said: "Is wrong, Rodrigo, how they mine, in a Dakota."

"In what way?"

"They follow a lode, yes?"

"You can't blame them for that."

"Follow a lode, and all a time, a tunnel, a crosscut, estope, all slide down a mountain—must one time come out in air, yes?"

"Looks like it."

"Real lode is dip."

"How you figure that out?"

"No figure, fill. Dees goddam owner, especially Hale, too chip to buy estoff he need to go dip. Try near top, follow liddle pocket, have a *bonanza* one day, bad *borrasca* next, all because no dig a mine in big way, in rill way, only liddle way, chip way."

"So?"

"Is old shaft up there, uphill, no?"

"The little one they abandoned?"

"We go down, try for big *bonanza*, dip under hill, yes?"

"I'll have a hell of a time with Williams."

"You tell, soon 'e have *borrasca*."

"How do you know?"

"You see. Soon no ore, only rock."

It came the next week, as a matter of fact. The vein began to narrow, and instead of a deep blue-black, the ore began to run a slaty gray, a blue-gray, a dull gray, and Hale was down there every half hour, breaking off specimens with his hammer and putting them in a box for the assayer. Then all of a sudden we were getting nothing but rock, and had to lay men off. That night I stopped by the office to talk with the super and lay it out what Paddy had said, and I thought he'd be sore when he found out I was handing him stuff I had got from a Mexican working in my gang. He wasn't.

"They're fine miners, the Mexican lads. They have a real skill with timber, and an instinct for metal. An instinct for a process and an instinct for a vein."

"He says the real ore's under the mountain."

"He's probably right."

"Then how about letting me dig?"

"Duval, I'm employed by Hale and I can tell you without hearing any more what he'll say. He'll agree with everything I tell him, roll his big black eyes, thank me for the suggestion, weep on me collar, open a bottle of rum—and do nothing. He thinks of costs, and the deep stuff is expensive."

"The *borrasca* is worst of all."

"So I've told him."

"And he'll wind up with no mine. You know what happens. They run *bonanza* a little while, then they run *borrasca* as long as they can, which means till they've spent the stake the *bonanza* piled up, and then some bank takes over."

"Stop talking about banks!"

We had it again that night, with Hale, at the International Hotel, and he did just like Williams said he would. He wept, and told us how his mother

101

was killed over in Hungary in 1848, and how much
he loved America, because it stood for liberty. He
said he didn't ask anything of anybody except jus-
tice. He said was it fair he had to pay four dollars
a day for his help when that very minute, for
roustabouts in St. Louis, they were paying twenty
cents an hour. It seemed to mean we couldn't do
what I wanted, so I said: "Will you let me prospect
just one entry? Off that small shaft that you abandoned last year? The one up the mountainside from
the big one we're using now?"

"It would cost too much."

"For what?"

"For hoist machinery. For gallows frames. For
cable. For men, for pumps, for everything."

"Suppose I do it for fifty dollars."

"For—how much?"

"In the first place, the guides have been left in,
for the lifting tub, and all we have to do is inspect
and repair, if repairs are needed. The old cable
was saved, and it's in good condition. It's old-time
hemp cable, but all I have to do is stretch it and
mark it. We got the old lifting tubs for that shaft,
in the shed, still right where they were stored. And

102

I won't need any gallows frame. I can do it with a gin pole."

"That means riggers, and—"

"Riggers? I'll rig it myself."

I told how many boats I'd rigged, and then I knew I had won, because his black rat eyes never left my face, and you could see him adding up figures and seeing where he was coming out. So next morning I was up the slope with Paddy and three helpers, and by night we had made plenty of progress. I didn't even have to move a winch up there. I used a spare one in the main hoisting works, cut a slot in the side of the building to let the cable through, and a little eye for my signal wire. I guyed the pole over the shaft, dropped a falls from the end of it, and to that attached my pulley. Pulleys are all different sizes, from the big ten- and twelve-footers over the big shafts, to smaller ones for different uses. The one I used was four feet. After it was in place and all safety attachments on the tub inspected, we dropped a man down, generally me or Paddy, to give signals, and when he was down we made a chalk mark on the cable at the drum. Then we pulled him up again, dropped him again, and marked again. At first we kept getting a three- or four-inch stretch, then we didn't get any. We marked with paint, then, a long red stripe to show the tub was 100 feet from the bottom, at the 600-foot level where we were going to dig. Then we marked a narrow white stripe for the stop.

The men did plenty of laughing, especially at the idea I could rig something, but Williams didn't and Hale didn't. They were around all the time, and when we started to work, Williams was signaling for the tub two or three times a day, and coming down, watching us move rock. We weren't sending any of it to the surface yet. Our tub wasn't fixed to take cars, and wouldn't be without considerable rebuilding. But we had room, on the platform where our entry met the shaft, to pile the rock we were taking out, so we could keep going in, first undercutting, then drilling, then shooting, then timbering, and then undercutting again. The big danger, of course, was the hot water, because while we had plenty of shaft for it to run into, we had no pump connected up, and if we hit a real gusher, it would mean everything below us would eventually be flooded, and ruin this part of the mine, whether we found anything or not. Williams kept feeling the face every time we'd shoot, for heat. One time he said to me: "Don't you find it warm, my lad, in that coat?"

"I don't like shirtsleeves."

"Could it be a gun you've got there?"

"It might be."

"I don't like it."

"They ganged on me once. They don't do it twice."

"One of the things that appealed to me about you, in addition to your education, was your size, and when you stretched Trapp on the rails, I was still more impressed with you. But a man with a gun impresses nobody. They're talking about it, and you've lost ground. They feel like convicts."

"They should have thought of that when they let me have it from behind. I felt like a sailor on the Shanghai water front. I'm wearing it awhile, if you don't mind."

"You'll regret it."

He wasn't the only one feeling the rock, and watching every crack and splinter in it like a hawk. Paddy was, and so were the other two Mexican miners we had with us, that could almost tell silver by inhaling. We shot down a face, and one of them picked up a hunk of red rock and began turning it over under his candle. It was cinnabar, the stuff they get quicksilver out of, and it didn't mean a thing, except we hadn't found ore of any kind since we'd been down here, and mercury and silver often go together. We mucked and timbered, and on the next shot Paddy got in there quick with his crowbar. He came out with something, and nothing was said, because it was soft and black, with the blue cast on it, and we all knew what it was. He rammed his bar in, got a boulder to rocking, and all of a sudden prized it out, so we had to jump to keep it from mashing our feet. And then here came the ore, just pouring out like a coke pile, where he kept ramming his bar into it and working it around. One of the Mexicans was the first to yell it: *"Bonanza!"*

Then the others were grinning and yelling and throwing their hats in the air, and even Paddy was showing his teeth, and Williams had that flinty smile on his face he didn't often show. "All right, my lads, we'll blow out for the day, and I'm recommending bonuses for all of you from Mr. Hale. It's fine, rich blue stuff, and I've no doubt in my mind we're in *bonanza* now, for quite a time."

We started for the tub, and Williams motioned me in first. But I hadn't forgotten whose idea it all was, and I stepped aside. "If it's all the same to you, sir, I'd like Paddy to have the honor. It was his doing, and I can go up with these other two."

"Padillo, get in."

"Yes, Señor Williams. *Viva la bonanza!*"

Williams pulled the signal wire, while the Mexicans screamed *bonanza* so I think they heard them on the moon, if anybody was up there, and the cable tightened, and the tub began to go up. Then it slammed down again. Both men hit their head on the side, and we jumped forward to help them out. Then Paddy began to yell, and we clawed hard, because something in his voice struck right into your belly. The cable was coming down, like some long strand of spaghetti, wrapping itself around both men, so every time we got them a little pulled over the edge, they were buried in cable again.

From above, in the shaft, there came a bumping, and then at last I understood this horrible thing Paddy was yelling at us. The pulley was coming down. I don't know how long it takes a four-foot wheel to fall six hundred feet, but it's an awful long time. And then nothing but the men's heads was showing above the coils of cable. And then the wheel struck. And then all over me and the other two Mexicans were the remains of what once had been men.

"All right, Mr. Hale, before we lock up for the night, and while we're still here in the office and nobody's around, why don't we get together on it, what we tell the grand jury tomorrow? So we don't get it all cock-eyed."

"Get together? The truth is all I know to tell."

"Which is?"

"Rigging."

"And whose fault was that?"

"Duval, why do you ask me that? I know, they all know, whose fault it was. I didn't want to go into that shaft. But you said leave it to you. You said you'd rig it because you'd rigged boats. Now look."

"The hoist engineer, he's got his own ideas."

"He couldn't see. I could."

"He don't like it, that you didn't holler."

"Or that you didn't."

"I'll deal with that little remark when I get around to it, but one thing at a time, as we're in a little bit of a hurry, as it wouldn't look so good if the two of us sat up here late, talking things over. The truth, you say, is all you know to tell, and that suits me too. Only one thing might keep me from it."

". . . What you mean, Duval?"

"Being made super."

"Here? In this mine?"

"That's it. The good old Dakota."

"First you rig the hoist so badly you kill two men, then you think I'll make you super? You must be crazy."

"I'm not so crazy."

"Then what are you getting at?"

"The stock."

". . . What stock?"

"Of this mine. Of the Dakota. That you bought

today. On the Stock Exchange. That you ran down and bid in before you ever made one move to get those bodies to the top or even find out what happened down there, though you say you saw the pulley gear go right down the shaft, and you must have known there were men under it."

"Is it against the law to buy stock?"

"No, it's legal."

"And how do you know about it?"

"I figured something like that might have happened, and went down there checking on it. It was no trouble to find out. The whole exchange was handing it to you, how you'd grabbed up the stock before news of the *bonanza* got out. It jumped eight points today, didn't it? Just before closing, when those bodies were being brought up, and the Mexicans told what they knew?"

". . . What else do you know, Duval?"

"About the axe."

"The—?"

"That you chopped at the cable with."

"The report says nothing about a chopped cable."

"That's right, you didn't chop any cable. You only chopped *at* it! Nobody was there, the hoist engineer couldn't see, because he was in the main hoisting works building, and then came this yell up the shaft. And then you thought fast, didn't you? They were hollering *bonanza*, and there was that axe still lying there, the one I used to trim up the gin pole. And you let fly with it, didn't you? Except that instead of chopping the cable you made a mislick and knocked the cable off the pulley. And when Ed shot the steam, it tore the pulley right off the axle and sent it and the cable and the tackle right down the shaft, didn't it?"

"I don't know anything about any axe."

"You think it just turned to steam on the way down? You think I didn't know what it meant when I saw it buried in Williams's head? You think I did it just because I liked blood when I put my arms around him and pulled it out and hid it so those Mexicans didn't see it? Come on, you son of a bitch, talk business or the grand jury's going to get that axe and the stock deal and everything else it'll take to send you to the gallows, and it won't be a gallows with pulley wheels under it, but one over a trap, with you in it, at the end of a rope."

"Now, Duval, don't talk like that—"

"I said super."

"Yes of course, Duval. You know, you're a young fellow, but we've had an eye on you ever since you came in this mine. I meant to make you super all along—"

"Write your notice."

". . . Sure thing. Absolutely."

"And that remark. About—"

"Is retracted."

"Then that's fine."

> *"Los enanitos*
> *Se enojaron,*
> *Porque a las enanas*
> *Les pellizcaron."*

I could hear him, out there in the night, and tears ran down my cheeks, for him and all the little people he loved so well, and for myself too, and how far I'd go, even to a blackmail game on his grave, to get something I ought to be ashamed even to want.

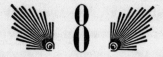

8

They raked me over the fire in the grand jury room till my face had blisters that felt like they'd last the rest of my life, because if there was no axe it was the rigging, and that meant me. But there was nothing I could be indicted for, like something willful, and I had my $600 a month, and that helped with the blisters. It was all over town, and if the men had despised me before, they hated me now. But I kept my gun on me always, and began weeding my mine. I mean, six or eight at a time, every Saturday night, I fired the men I had been miners with, and took on new ones, mostly men that had arrived a few days before and didn't know me from Adam. Hale paid no attention, because we were making plenty of changes, moving from the big shaft in four compartments to the little one where the strike was. I used special cages I had made, with three decks for cars, so we wouldn't have to slow down to enlarge the shaft, and specially so we wouldn't be enlarging it on bank money, but on our own, after we made some from the strike.

Then came the day when I was rid of all the miners that were sore at me, except Olesen, the big Swede, and Gator, the fellow that claimed he was a flat boat man, and would jump up and crack his heels and say his grandpappy was an alligator, and let on he was tough. It was Saturday, and they were to get it that night, and I could tell they knew it. How they found out I don't know, but in a mine the timekeeper has a wife or a girl or something, and everybody knows what goes on practically before it happens. I could tell, from the way they were just pretending to work, there on the loading platform, rolling on cars, that they'd been told. And then all of a sudden, while I was leaning against a square set, waiting for the next car to come down, it was like some bee had stung me, only a lot worse.

I looked, and a candlestick was through my hand, pinning it to the timber.

A candlestick is like a clay pipe made out of iron, with the stem part a sharp point that they stick in wood or in dirt wherever they want a light, the bowl a cup that holds the butt of the candle, and the nub a curlicue that comes around and under, so they can hook a finger in it and yank it out as easy as they stuck it in. I reached for the curlicue with my good hand, but I didn't catch it. Because a six-pound striking hammer swung past my head, and the breeze put out the candle in my hat, and the jolt put out the candle on the stick. And then there I was in the dark, with that candlestick driven so deep in the wood I couldn't get it out no matter how I pulled with my free hand, and the hot wax spilling down and mixing with the blood, and still I couldn't get loose. "Get his gun!"

"His gun, hell, get his guts!"

They kicked me and beat me and did their best to get my gun, but I used my teeth and it stayed under my arm, even if I couldn't get it out to use it. Maybe I hollered. Anyway there was plenty of noise, and pretty soon there were lights up the entry, where other miners were on their way, running. But before they got there Gator jumped on the cage, pulled Oleson aboard, and gave the signal. He and the boy were up to the top by the time they prized me loose.

They got me to the top at last, and took me to a doctor on Taylor Street. It wasn't bleeding much, but it was all mashed and raw, and hurt like holy hell. The doctor was named Rausch, and if he was a regular doctor or a horse doctor I don't know, but the way he treated me it felt like he thought I was a horse. He poured a liniment over it that he made from mixing whisky and witch hazel in a bottle, like it was a salad dressing, and then he bandaged it up with rags he tore up from women's petticoats he had in one drawer of his desk. When he got done I was so weak I could hardly stagger, and he got sore when I asked him to call a cab, but I hadn't taken the gun off and when I begun fingering it with my left hand he went outside, and pretty soon a cab was there.

Next day I went to work, but by noon I felt so queer I had to come up and sit down in the office. Hale kept watching me, and pretty soon said I ought to go home. He didn't send me, he took me, in his own carriage, and didn't leave until I was in bed, and another doctor had come, a young fellow that at least acted like I was human. It wasn't like Hale at all, but I figured out why he was so kind. I was out of my head a little, and he was afraid I'd talk.

How long I lay there I don't know, but Mrs. Finn would come, and the doctor, and every time he washed my hand and bandaged it, it made me sicker to look at it, because it was swelled up the size of a ham and about the same color. And then one afternoon they were all in there, Hale and Mrs. Finn and the doctor, and the Chinese cook bringing hot water, and a look on their faces that said they were up to something. The doctor opened his case and got out a bottle of whisky and some tools. He poured me a tumbler full and told me to drink it. I put down a swallow or two, and gagged on it. "What the hell is it for? Ain't I sick enough already without a bellyful of this stuff?"

"You'll need it."

"What for?"

"For what I've got to do to you."

"And what's that?"

". . . Take off your arm."

"Oh no you're not."

"Duval, you've got blood-poisoning. I've done everything I know to prevent it, and nothing I've done has helped. There's only one thing left, and that's an amputation. The alternative is, if we don't resort to that, and resort to it now, while there's still time, or we hope there's still time, in three more days you'll be dead. Now let's not deceive ourselves. Removal of an arm is a major operation, and one hell of a painful one. You've got one little thing in your favor, on that score. You've had practically nothing in your stomach since day before yesterday, and I think this liquor is going to put you out pretty completely. I'm not going to start till you've had a lot, but it's going to be bad. You may as well be prepared."

"I won't let you."

118

"I tell you, you're going to die."

"Then all right."

But next thing I knew he was washing my arm, and Hale was shoving the whisky bottle against my teeth, and Mrs. Finn was standing by, with a basin. I knocked the bottle away with my chest and kicked the basin out of Mrs. Finn's hands. The doctor began to cuss at me. "Goddam it, we're trying to save your life, and the least you can do is act like you had sense."

"Nobody asked you to save it."

"Well, we're going to."

He motioned with his hand, and two miners stepped up, that I hadn't seen before, and began tying me down, with rope. I fought and they fought back. I screamed at Hale, told him he'd be better off if I was dead, on account of what I knew, and why didn't he make them let me alone? He screamed back, and I got the point a little bit then. Paddy and Williams had been paying him a few visits at night and he had just prayed them out of there when now I'd be teaming up with them, and the three of us, he figured, would really be tough. So he helped tie. And then all of a sudden they let

go, and she was standing there, and my heart gave
the same jump it had given in Sacramento, because
she had that same look on her face, and I knew
neither they nor fifty more like them could do anything to me now, because she wouldn't let them.
How she got there I didn't at that time know, but it
was easy to figure, later on. The house entrance was
on B Street, but you climbed stairs in a long tunnel
of a staircase to the rooms, which backed up on A.
The boardwalk ran right past the window of my
room, and she had just stepped off it to the sill, and
then to the floor.

She looked things over, and said: "Thanks ever
so much, doctor, for what you're doing to Roger,
but I'll take charge of him from now on, if you
don't mind."

"And who are you?"

"Just a friend."

"Do you know what this man has the matter with
him?"

"I see it's his hand. I'm curing him up."

"Not in my house you're not."

That was Mrs. Finn, who had been looking
Morina over. One of the miners or somebody must

have whispered something, because she cut loose with a spiel that sounded like something she had learned up for church, all about the respectable house she ran, and how nobody like Morina could come in it, even over her dead body. She was one of those dumb, worked-out women that naturally has it hard no matter where she goes. She had run a lunchroom for rivermen in St. Louis before she married Finn and came with him to the minefields. He put down so much booze she got religion, and after he died in Grass Valley she came on to Nevada and opened up the same old rivermen's joint, except here it was miners.

She was hooking it up good when Morina stepped over to her, her hips swinging and her eyes showing that same cold glitter I'd seen there before. Right in the middle of a holler Mrs. Finn broke off, and when the doctor wigwagged her she went out in the hall with him and for a whole minute they were whispering to each other, while Morina looked from one to the other in the room, trying to figure out what was being said. When they came back Mrs. Finn nodded to the doctor, and he did the talking. "You're willing to assume responsibility for this man, knowing as I now warn you that his injury will probably prove fatal unless he submits to the surgery I have recommended?"

"I told you once I am."

"You know you're not allowed out of this room?"

"If that fool says so, it's her house."

"You'll provide him with what he needs?"

"I will."

"You—"

"I'll put you out if you don't go. Now git."

By that time she had spotted my gun, where I kept it, hanging by the straps to a bedpost. She walked over, unstrapped it, let it swing over her arm. They got out of there fast, and when they were gone she hung the gun up again and came over to the bed. "Roger, I got to tell you something."

"How'd you know what they were up to?"

"Oh, things get around."

"You mean you keep track of me?"

"My little piece of live bait, I got to watch him."

"You mean you love me?"

"I mean I got something to tell you."

"Then tell it."

"I know a salve I can make."

"I need it, God knows."

"It's a conjure salve, Roger."

"All right."

"You know what that is, a conjure salve?"

"If you make it, it's all right with me. I know you won't let me die. And if I do die, I'll know, from how you came here today, that you love me."

"Conjure, that's in cahoots with the devil."

"I said all right."

"It's like you pray that somebody gets well, only you pray to the devil, and you got to give him a live snake, and then while you pray you got to put the snake in the salve, and then you get well."

I thought a long time about that, if you can say you think when your ears are ringing with fever, and your hand is pounding like a sledge hammer was mashing it up, and you're so sick you want to throw up even when you haven't got anything to throw up. It seemed so funny, that no sooner she did something that made me want to stand up and cheer, and brought me so close to her it seemed we were made to be together, than here would come this other thing, this side of her that was sin, or evil, or whatever you'd want to call it. If a snake went in

123

the salve, what did I care? I'd eaten five hundred eels that I caught off Bay Ridge, and that part meant nothing to me. But what kind of Louisiana swamp drip did she have in her blood that made her get the devil in it? Once more I said all right, but for one second it swept over me to tell her no, I'd die before I had any part of the devil, because even if I didn't believe he was there, she did, and that made it wrong.

What woke me was a drum-beat, and when I opened my eyes it was night, and there by the washstand was the biggest, blackest man I had ever seen, with a broken nose that was mashed flat all over his face, nothing on from the waist up, and a little drum in front of him, made from a gourd with a skin stretched over it, that he kept touching with the tips of his fingers. Later I found out he was named Scott, and was the husband of Mattiny, the cook down at the house on D Street. In a minute she stepped through the window, just as black as he was, with a red tignon over her head and big gold rings in her ears, and carrying a pot. She crossed the room, and all of a sudden her face was in the

124

light, and I noticed the smell of rock oil. I looked, and there on the floor, kneeling in front of a big lamp, was Biloxi, whispering to herself, and motioning for the pot. Mattiny set it on top of the lamp, on a little attachment that held things that were to be heated. Then Biloxi closed her eyes and began waving her hands.

Outside, a board creaked in the hall. I opened my mouth to tell them to watch out, somebody was out there, probably the whole damned boarding house. But Mattiny went over and listened, so they knew about it.

I must have gone under again, because next thing I knew a chill was going up my back like cold feathers had tickled it, from a sound in the room you'll never forget if you hear it once, and in that God-awful country you hear it often: the rattle of a rattlesnake. It's dry, like the rustle of old leaves, but it gets louder, and all of a sudden it's going right into your belly, or wherever you keep your guts. I opened my eyes, and across the ring of light on the ceiling something was waving. I looked toward the lamp, and Morina's face was right over it, white, and screwed up hard. The pot I couldn't see and her hands I couldn't see, but then came a hiss and the bang of a pot lid, and for three seconds the roar of all hell boiling. Then it was quiet, and her face relaxed, and she nodded. Mattiny came into the light beside her, and lifted off the pot.

"Roger."

"Yes, Morina."

"This is going to hurt."

"Then send them away, Biloxi and the others. I can't stand much more. If I bawl or something, I don't mind if it's only you, but I don't want anybody else to see it."

"There's nobody here but me."

"Then go ahead."

"It has to go on hot."

"If that's all, I'll be all right."

"Boiling hot."

"I won't mind."

I almost hit the ceiling when she put it on, a whole big gob of it in the middle of the cloth, but I clenched my teeth and didn't holler. When it was bound on tight it got worse, and she held my head to her breast, and I could feel her tears falling down over my cheek. After it had been on a few minutes it had to be changed, and each time was worse than the last, and each time she held me to her was sweeter than the last, and I could feel it stronger, the way she loved me. And then one time after she bound on some more of it, my hand gave three or four throbs, like a knife had been stuck in it, and I told her I thought something had happened. She took off the bandage and washed off the salve, and looked. Then she told me to double up my hand as far as I could. Before I half moved my fingers it squirted across and hit the wall. "That's it, Roger! That's what it wanted!"

"Christ, but it stinks."

"Never mind the stink, let it come!"

She bathed it and squeezed it and pulled strings out of it all that day. And then around sundown the pain, the fever, and the fear were all gone, and I sank down in a deep, wonderful sleep.

Around dawn I was thirsty, and reached out to pour myself a drink of ice water from the pitcher she had set on a little bench beside the bed. She came over and did it, and held the glass while I drank, and sat down and felt my head. "You slept nine hours."

"I feel so much better."

"Your hand hurt?"

"None any more. It's better. I can feel it."

"Later on I'll bandage it."

"Tough on you."

"Oh, I'm all right. I caught some sleep in the chair, and Biloxi's feeding me wonderful. Your breakfast'll be along directly."

"What do you call this dress?"

"Gingham."

"Never saw you in that before."

"I've been working."

"Makes you look like a young girl."

She smoothed my pillow and patted my cheek and gave me a little kiss on the forehead. I put my arm around her and half pulled her down beside me. We lay that way a long time, she running her fingers through my hair, me touching her and smell-

128

ing her and feeling how warm and soft she was. I kissed her on the cheek, just a little brush of a kiss. She didn't pull away, but she didn't come closer either. I kissed her again, a little nearer the mouth. "No."

"Just one."

"If you ask for more, I'll move."

I kissed her, then held her tight and kissed her again, and again after that. I could feel her lips get hot under mine. "Roger, I don't want you to kiss me that way."

"Why not? We love each other, don't we?"

"I've told you why not."

I held her tighter, and her lips got hotter, and I knew I was going to have her. But when I did, she cried, and kept on crying.

9

When he found out he could trust me, Hale wanted me back, because things went sour under the new super, and he felt I brought him good luck. That was why he worked on Mrs. Finn that I could stay there, and told her Morina was just a girl I had known back home, and I wouldn't be surprised he said she was my cousin. Anyhow, I didn't have to look up any new place, and he began making the best propositions I ever had, beginning with a raise, and maybe some stock, and whatever I had in mind. But those three or four weeks, when I needed a new bandage every day, I had gone down to D Street, and when I didn't mention what had happened, she didn't, and we'd sit on the back porch in the afternoon, and look down at the trees in the flats four or five miles away, the only patch of green you could see anywhere around. And sometimes Biloxi would sit with us, and if Renny came out there they'd talk French, but mostly he stayed inside and practiced the piano. The square one was gone now, and a big grand was in its place. Sometimes Haines would come over, and if he was sober, and they were doing Italian selections with high notes in them, he could shoot a nice piece of silver, I'll say that for him. And the other girls would come out there, but I didn't care much for them. Two or three of them, Reiner's Mexican girl Lola, Chinchin the half-Chinese girl, and Pat Kelly the New York chorus girl, were pretty enough, but dumber than hell and they fought a lot. I was with Morina, though, that was the main thing, and I'd try to forget what went on at night, and for an hour or two be happy. In her room was a photograph of an hombre in uniform, and when I asked who he was she said: "My husband." It was the first I knew she'd been married to a Venezuelan general in Caracas, and only came to Virginia City when he got killed in a street fight.

But I wanted those afternoons, and if I went back

with Hale I couldn't have them. I kept thinking about my shooting, and one evening I went back to the same old gully to see how it felt to use a gun again. But at the first shot, what that stock did to the palm of my hand almost knocked me over with pain. The next night, though, I tried it with a little leather guard I had a shoemaker make me, and it was better, though the gun popped off it like a pickle off a fork. When I got a little soft leather pad, and a strap to hold it in place, I could hardly feel anything at all, and I began the same old schedule I'd followed before, popping at playing cards to start off with, and then when the rabbits came out, drawing and wheeling and firing at them, for speed. In a week or two I was as good as I ever was, and marched myself down to the Esperanza, one of the big gambling halls on C Street, the morning after the lookout quit, on account of a little trouble with a dissatisfied customer, horizontally. The proprietor was named Rocco, the son of an Italian charcoal-burner on the Sierra. He didn't pay much attention when I applied for the job. "You look a little young to me, son."

"It's a young fool's job, isn't it?"

"It's a shooting job."

"Anything around here you particularly want shot?"

"Out back, as it happens, there is."

"Then let's go out back."

"I'll get you a gun."

"I might have one, if I looked."

He tried to see where I was carrying it, but by now it lay so snug you could hardly see it. He led the way out back, and tiptoed to a privy that had a board fence running back of it and a lattice built around it. Then he picked up a rock and heaved and it hit the privy like a grenade or something. Three rats jumped out the backside of it, and began running along the bottom of the board fence toward a pile of crates in one corner. I plugged them before they'd gone five feet. He stared at the bunches of blood and fur that were kicking around, and then he turned to me, but by now I had the gun back in the holster. ". . . You spit that stuff, or what?"

"That's it, pardner."

"You that good on a man?"

"When I'm scared, I'm fast."

"I'll take a chance, I think."

"What's the pay, by the way?"

"Fifteen a day, and you work at night."

"I hear you pay twenty."

"To the right man, yes."

"I'm checking in tonight."

"You wear a black suit. I require that."

In the West a gambler wears the black suit, and some places even have the lookout do it. I said it was all right, I'd have one on, and he said: "And I'd get a haircut if I were you. I hear some of those generals at the Battle of Gettysburg wore curls right up to the mouth of the cannon, but anybody that tries it in my place is going out on his ear."

"And anybody that tries to cut mine is going out in a box. Have we got that matter straight?"

"Well, don't get excited."

"So it's understood."

I wasn't wearing curls. I had been sick, and neglected to get a haircut, that was all. But I wasn't having him telling me, so that's how I combed them out the way the girls wear them in school. Mine are yellow and curly, and all next afternoon, out on the back porch, I could feel Morina looking at me out the corner of her eye, when I showed up in the black velvet suit with silver buttons, the stitched boots, the black felt hat, the red shirt, and nice gold curls rippling around on my collar. I kept figuring what I'd say if she started to laugh at me, and I had a joke figured up. But once our eyes crossed, and I saw she wasn't laughing. Then a throb went through my mouth, and I knew she liked how I looked. I picked her up, carried her inside, and pushed my face against hers. It was hot, and couldn't lie to me about what it wanted. She didn't lie. She just fought me, bit me, kicked me, and threw me out.

Two or three nights later, I found out what I'd do when it wasn't just target practice. I don't know if you know how it works in a gambling hall. On one side is the bar, pretty long, with a brass rail and three or four men mixing drinks. At both ends are the big fixtures, wheels of fortune and stuff like that, that run straight up and down and have mirrors and pictures and gaudy stuff all over them. Opposite the bar is faro, with four or five layouts,

135

girls dealing at each table. On one side of the faro are dice games, like crap, and on the other side cards. In the middle of the room, between the bar and the faro, are three big roulette tables, each running a different limit. My place was up front, in the corner between the wheels of fortune and the dice, and for the purpose of seeing better I sat in a high chair. The lookout's high chair is not any different from a baby's high chair, and it works on the same principle, with a cross bar for your heels, arm rests, and everything else, but of course with no attachment to come down over your head and get in the way of free movement.

I was sitting there, getting used to my job, which was to keep an eye on things, and in case I saw something peculiar, like maybe a pair of dice coming out of a coattail, to drift over and walk past the gambler on that table. Those hombres, they don't need any assay report to know there's quicksilver in the ivory, so there was nothing exciting about it, and the only time I was to do something quick was in case of real trouble. So this night a fellow was at the bar, putting down liquor. I noticed him because it seemed to me he was working at it, and besides he was wearing two .44's, butts facing. I mean, the gun on his left hip hung for his right hand, and the one on the right hip for his left. And then all of a sudden he grabbed for his guns and gave a one-man demonstration of all the things the fellow in the store had told me not to do. His right-hand gun came out first, and he shot with it, but a hip-shot that caused one of the comicalest things you ever saw. The gun went off, but it yanked him off balance, so he had to let go the other gun and grab for the bar to keep from falling. What he thought he was doing I don't know, but as well as I could figure it out later he thought he'd pop off a few times so everybody would dive for the floor, and then he'd scoop up some money and run. Or maybe he thought he was shooting at me with that first one. From the hip, it could have been anything, and if it didn't make sense there was no law it had to.

Anyway, as he reached for his guns I was drawing mine. It never seems to come out quick. It's a year before it's clear, and you think you'll lose your mind before you bring the sights into line, and when you fire you're like a wild man to line it up again. But in this case it was like I was taking my time and doing a nice, refined job. The .44 yanked his arm up and over, and as he lurched against the bar I had plenty of time to aim, and even to change my mind. Instead of shooting for his heart I popped one in his shoulder. Then as that gun dropped I broke his collar bone on the left side, so he wouldn't get ambitious with the other gun. The place was screaming like a million hyenas were in it, but he stood there blinking like a man in a dream, and looked at the deputies when they collared him like he couldn't imagine where he was. Then the whole place swarmed over him, and I think he'd have been lynched if the officers hadn't hustled him out, yelling at me to stay where I was, they'd let me know when they needed me.

I never had so many free drinks, cigars, and chips out of roodle pots thrown at me in twenty minutes in my life. I had plugged a poor loon and I was the hero of the town. Even the two writers for the *Enterprise* were all over me, and they decided I was the greatest gun fighter in the West, because I didn't even *have* to kill my man. I just winged him, and they said that was a novelty, and refreshing. To me, they looked like a pair of crazy newspaper men that would do anything to make people laugh. Anyway, that's how it came out in the paper, and overnight I was an important man in Virginia City.

"So you were going to save the Confederacy and help the boys in gray and now you're a goddam paid gunman in a Nevada gambling sink all dressed in black velvet like a Mexican cowboy with yellow curls over your collar and in love with a whore that's not worth the powder it would take to blow her to hell."

You lie awake enough, you talk to yourself.

10

All that time I had heard plenty about Brewer, and seen her with him, though after what she had said I would have put my eyes out before I'd have let her catch me looking, so when they came down the street I generally ducked around the corner. She drove a pair of black ponies to a small buggy, and the ponies had silver buckles on their harness, and the whole town knew he had given them to her. So one day, when I pulled the bell at 17, and a strange woman answered and said Biloxi had moved to the new house being built on A Street, I knew without being told what was up. When I went up there painters were still working on the shutters, and furniture was piled all over the big high portico with pillars on it that ran clear up to the second floor. Biloxi opened the door and took me in her arms and kissed me and called me her *pauvre petit* and took me inside.

There was a wide hall running from the front door to a winding staircase, and big rooms with high windows in them on each side. In one room there was nothing but the grand piano from D Street, and Renny in front of it, playing. Until then he never noticed me that I recall now, but when he saw me he jumped up and shook hands and began to rave about the room. He said the acoustics were so wonderful you couldn't believe it, and he was never going to put any more furniture in it, except shelves for the music and a bench running around for people to sit on. Sofas, rugs, and pillows, he said, were out. He could hardly wait for Haines, and pretty soon Haines showed up, and sang some grand opera. Then Biloxi made him sing her some songs in French, and rang for Mattiny to put out drinks. Then she brought me to a room across the hall, where anyway a sofa had been put in and you could sit. "Ah Roger, it is ze happiest day of my life! George is soch wonderful man!"

"Brewer?"

"Morina's fiancé."

"Oh, they're going to be married?"

"Yes at last. And soch beautiful thing he has done for me. This house, all summer he build, as surprise for me. And now today, he move me in — pouf, like that, after breakfast."

"Why?"

"He love Morina. He is like brozzer to me."

"Hell of a friendly brother. And a hell of a place."

"Twenty rooms, Roger, big rooms."

"Where are the girls?"

"Girls? Roger! I have no girls here!"

"No business here?"

"Business, *fini!*"

"His idea?"

"He want his little Biloxi to have easy."

"Makes a little more sense that way."

"But Roger, he is *rich!*"

"He certainly must be proud."

I asked when the wedding was to be, and she said in a couple of weeks, as soon as Morina got back from San Francisco, where she was going to-night to buy clothes. She began rattling the ice in her glass and looking at the little watch she had pinned to her dress. She had spilled her news and had her cry, and wanted me to go. Me, I wasn't quite ready.

It was late afternoon when I heard horses, slipping and sliding, climbing Union Street. It was the ponies, and behind them a hack, and Morina waited for the hackman to hitch before she came inside. The buggy was too small for trunks, so the idea seemed to be he would take them to Overland, while Biloxi drove her down. The stage left at six, so there was quite a lot of running around, and for a few minutes she didn't take any notice of me. Then all of a sudden she came into the room, closed the door, lit a *cigarrillo,* and sat down beside me. While she was upstairs she had changed into the same little traveling dress she had worn when I first saw her, with the same little bonnet. She took two or three inhales before she said anything, and during that time she didn't look at me. Then: "Did Biloxi tell you about me, Roger?"

"She said you were getting married."

"I want you to wish me well."

"I will on one condition."

"What's that, Roger?"

"That you tell me, in some way that I respect, why you're marrying this man instead of me, when I've asked you a hundred times, and I ask you one more time right here and now."

"I can't throw away a chance like this."

"Like what?"

"Why, Roger, George is a millionaire."

"Is money all you think about?"

"Doesn't everybody?"

"They don't do to get it what you do to get it. You've sold yourself for it, you've made a public spectacle of yourself for it, you've led a life of shame for it, not because you had to, because I'd have taken you off D Street any time, but because that money and that life was what you wanted. And now you're marrying this man, not because you love him, but because he's got a mine over there that's making him so much money he can't count it. I don't call that being a wife. I call it being the highest-priced whore in the state of Nevada, and I'll see you in hell before I wish you well at it."

144

"Something might happen to you for that."

"Nothing will."

"Don't be too sure."

"There's nothing I'd like better than to drill you through your dirty little heart, and I could do it right now, so if anything starts happening around here you know who it's going to happen to."

"How do you know whether I love him?"

"Because you love me."

"Not that way."

"There's only one way."

"Anyway, he loves me, I know that."

"How?"

"Look what he's given me."

"When they buy you, that proves love?"

"What other way can a man show how much he thinks of you, if he don't give you things? What have you ever given me?"

"Don't you know why they pay to have you?"

"Because they want me."

"So you can't have them."

"That don't mean anything I can understand."

"It means that after it's over they can walk out and you've got no claim on them or right to say any part of them was ever yours or even the right to speak to them on the street. No, I never gave you anything, but myself, and that's why I'm up here right now—"

Tears began running down her face, and she beat on the sofa with her fists. "It's not true, what you're saying! When a man gives you something, it proves how *popular* you are! It didn't have to be me. It could have been any girl on the street. But instead of them, he finds me attractive, and the way he shows it, he gives me a present. And when it's a nice present, a big present, it's a *wonderful* compliment!"

I guess she said more, but all I remember is the way her eyes shone through the tears, and the way it hit me in the stomach, to find out at last *why* she was what she was. To her it was living. It was like being a queen, of a tiny, miserable, rotten little kingdom maybe, but with a crown on her head just the same.

That night came news of Chickamauga, and I don't know which felt worse, me or the town. Because if it was the biggest thing for the South since Chancellorsville, there was nothing I had done to make me feel I had a part of it. And if the town was Union, there were plenty by now that were beginning to wonder if they'd ever get their war won, which of course they won't. There wasn't much whooping in the saloons that night, especially in the Esperanza, where the high-class trade took a thing like that a lot more to heart than a place with nothing but a bunch of bums at the bar. They stood around by twos and threes, talking it over, and not very loud. All you could hear was Bragg, Bragg, and Bragg. One day before, he'd been the funniest object on earth. They'd made jokes about his name, his looks, and his rows with his generals. Now they mumbled about him like he was a cross between Napoleon Bonaparte and a she grizzly, and nothing could stop him.

So out back, where I'd gone for some air, a little more mumbling didn't mean anything, at first. It was on the other side of the fence, a few feet from where I was leaning against the building, looking at the stars, and I just figured it was a few more lads that had found out that hoping to win a war was not quite the same as winning it. But then all of a sudden I woke up. This had nothing to do with war. It was about a little party that was to start in a few minutes, and the guest of honor was to be me. There seemed to be four of them, but the only name I caught was Hoke. I didn't know at that time that he was Big Hoke Irving, known from Texas to Canada as one of the worst bad men in the West. He laid it out for them three times. At nine o'clock they were to drift in one at a time and he'd take position near the door. One of the others was to go to the bar, order a drink, and at Hoke's handkerchief signal begin to shoot. I was the first target, and after I dropped, he was to shoot at lights, bottles, and anything that would make a noise and scare the crowd. Hoke was to holler at them and shoot at anything that made trouble, but mainly huddle them and get them on the floor. When he gave the word, the other two were to go down the line with a gunny sack one of them had under his coat, and grab everything in sight, one holding the sack, the other scooping money. But the main thing, he said, was do it fast and do it rough. If they did

it right, they'd be in, out, and away less than five
minutes after they started.

I held my breath, and when they moved off I
raised on tiptoe to look, but next door was a vacant
lot with no lights or anything, and all I could see
was shadows. I went inside to warn Rocco and tell
him what I thought we should do, which was to get
deputies and get them quick. But when I started
over to him, where he was talking to some officers
near my chair, I stopped. Because coming into the
place, with Red Caskie, the fellow that did his er-
rands, his brother Raymond, that had charge of all
chemical operations at his mine, and three or four
hombres from his office, was Brewer. My head began to pound. I went over to my chair and sat down,
but instead of saying something to Rocco I looked
at the clock. It was twenty minutes to nine.

Once you saw him, the idea that Brewer could
love anybody, unless it was himself, was nothing
more or less than funny. He was good-looking
enough, in a heavy kind of way, and always had a

grin and wave of the hand for whoever came along, but just the same he wasn't romantic. He wasn't as tall as I am, but he was at least six feet, with a big barrel chest and a rolling walk they said he got from being a lumberman, up in Wisconsin. Anyway, making all the money he had came from all the stuff he knew about timber. Up to a few months ago almost anybody that could timber a mine so it wouldn't cave in and kill everybody down there could get rich in Virginia City, and he was thick with Deidesheimer, who taught them how to make squaresets, so right at the start he had a big advantage. Then he brought his brothers in, who were in some college back east, and sent them to work for a bank, and after they learned all they could about processes and finances, they came back with him again. Then Will went to San Francisco, to deal with the mint and the silver-buyers, and Raymond took charge of the mill. But when it came to George, it affected him the way it would affect any dumb lumberman from the north woods that made about ten times as much money as he ever thought he would have. He got this idea that only the best was good enough for him, whether it was food, drink, or cigars, and if you ask me, the main thing he saw in Morina was that she could pile on more clothes, diamonds, and ribbons than any other woman in town, so of course that made her the best, and the way he figured things out, the perfect wife.

He began rapping on the bar with his cane, and ordered up champagne for everybody in the house. Jake had a grin all over his face, and began yelling at Ike and Davey to fill the ice tub, to open cases, to get out the extra glasses in the closet. But when he got out a bottle and held it for Brewer, it wasn't good enough. Brewer smashed it down on a beer tap, and told him to get some real champagne, and me, I don't know one champagne from another, but a funny look come over Jake's face. I can't prove it, but I'd bet the champagne Brewer paid for that night wasn't as good as the champagne he slopped on the floor.

Rocco was all grin too, and motioned all dealers and croupiers to close down their games. So the whole mob, except me, crowded to the bar. Caskie came over. "What's the matter, Rog, don't you feel sociable?"

"I'm supposed to stay sober."

"George, he wants you."

"Tell him thanks, but tonight I'm off it."

"Listen, there's not many hombres in this town that's too goddam busy to step over to the bar when George Brewer wants to buy them a drink."

"I'm on duty."

"Listen, Rog, that's what he's in here for."

"To get me drunk?"

"He knows about you."

"What's he know?"

"About you and Morina."

"He don't know much, if that's all."

"And about Hale too. He knows all about that, and he's liked you ever since. He thinks it was pretty damn nice, the way you treated that hombre, and he wants to buy you a drink."

"Well, that's different."

"That sounds more like it."

"Tell him soon as I finish my nine o'clock round, I'll be over, but I'd rather he started the others off first, so if we want to talk, we can do it quiet and not have a lot of whooping and hollering going on account he's put out free drinks."

"He'll like you for that, Rog."

152

I wasn't taking his drink, but if he came in there to buy me one and I turned it down, he might plunk down his money and walk out. That wouldn't do for what I had in mind.

At seven of, the first bottle came out of the ice, where Ike had been twirling it and feeling if it was cold enough. Jake cut the wire, the cork hit the ceiling, and foam spilled out. Glasses were lined up on the bar for ten feet now, dozens and dozens of them, and Jake began filling them. Davey cut another wire, another cork popped, and Jake took the second bottle. Eighteen or twenty glasses were ready, and Brewer picked up one. "To the Union, one and indivisible forever!"

" 'Ray!"

They began to yell and drink. But they crowded around him too, and for me that was bad. I got my high chair and took it to Rocco. "Maybe, tonight at least, we could find a place for Mr. Brewer to sit."

Rocco ran over with it and Brewer raised his glass to me like he was some kind of duke and I bowed back as elegant as I could. Then he climbed up on it and hooked his heels over the foot rest. He was a head and a half above the crowd. As Jake refilled his glass a slim man in a red shirt, with two guns on his hips, came in. He blinked when he saw the celebration, but Rocco went over, handed him a glass, and said all drinks were on Mr. Brewer, so drink his health. Brewer raised his glass at him, and he nodded with a quick, pale grin and took a sip. Then he drifted over to the edge of the crowd. He was facing Brewer, but his eyes began running over the room. When he saw me, he shifted his glass from his right hand to his left. I took a stroll down the room, past the croupiers counting money, and as I moved he turned. When I stopped at the dollar table and gave the wheel a spin, he was between me and Brewer, about six feet from me and the same distance from the chair, with the three of us right in line. The clock said one minute of.

Two men came in wearing guns, one of them with his coat buttoned tight. They had a hangdog

look to them, and Rocco, instead of handing them a
drink, came over to me. "Roger—"

"I'm watching every move they make."

"All right, boy."

"And stay away from Red Shirt."

"Him too?"

"I think so."

At nine a big man came in, with a red beard
and both hands in his coat pockets. He took a quick
look at the room, spotted first the two that had just
come in, then Red Shirt over near the bar. Then he
whipped a red handkerchief out of one pocket. Red
Shirt reached for his gun, the one on his left hip
with reversed stock, and got it out. But I drew with
the handkerchief too, and before he could shoot I
plugged him, through the head. And while he was
falling I shot again, for the place where his head
had been, and Brewer pitched over. After that it
was like one of those lantern slides, where the boy
chases the butterfly to the end of the pier, then falls
in to the fishes, but it takes six pictures to show what
happened in one second. I threw myself backward

over the roulette table and rolled, and when I hit
the floor I had three tables between me and the men
near the door. The big man was already shooting
for me, and I shot at him once and missed. I had to
get closer, and ran on my knees and one hand up
toward the front, and he was doing the same on the
other side of the tables, to get me. He raised up and
I shot again and he dropped. I turned toward the
other two. I only had two shots left and I couldn't
waste anything. But they were legging it for the
door. I got one of them in the back as he started
through the door. The other one I got outside, as he
was jumping on his horse. It went galloping down
the street with him hanging to one stirrup.

"Duval, who killed George Brewer?"

"That I don't know."

"Don't trifle, boy. Who killed him?"

"I heard what the doctor said, what Mr. Rocco
said, what these other witnesses said. They say I
shot twice at this unidentified man, and that one of
those shots killed Mr. Brewer. They say I took cover
back of the roulette equipment then, and shot the

big man Hoke Irving. They say I got the little man as he was leaving, and the other one outside. So I guess if anybody killed Mr. Brewer, it had to be me. But if I leave guessing out and tell it like I remember it, all I know is this man here started to draw and I started to shoot. From there on I've got no clear recollection of anything until I saw that horse go running down the street, and I never even knew Mr. Brewer was dead until I got back inside. Nobody regrets it more than I do. But I'm under oath to tell you the truth, and I'm telling it as well as I can. And I'm certainly not trifling with you."

"That all you got to say?"

"Yes sir, it is."

It was the City Marshal, and he started his inquest as soon as the wagon came back with the man the horse had dragged down the street. First he put me under arrest and detailed a deputy to guard me. Then he picked six men out of the crowd to serve as a coroner's jury. Then he sent for the same doctor that wanted to cut off my arm. Then he told everybody to hold up their right hand and swear that the evidence they would give before him would be the truth, the whole truth, and nothing but the truth. Then he began examining witnesses, first the doctor, to get him to pronounce the dead men dead, and tell what they died of. Then Raymond Brewer, to identify his brother. Then a whole flock of people, practically everybody in the place, and a fellow that had just got in a few days ago from Nebraska got all excited when he identified Hoke Irving, but nobody had names for the other three. Then he had all five bodies laid out in front of the bar, and drew over them one of the oilcloth covers for the roulette tables. Then he began taking testimony. He was cold, tough, cold, and official with everybody, and you couldn't tell what his opinion was, if he had one. When I got done, he asked the jury if there were any questions they wanted to ask, and after some stuff they got me to explain, about where I was when the shooting started, where Irving was, and where I took cover, he told them to consider their verdict. They whispered a minute or two, and then the one he had appointed foreman got up and said: "We the jury empaneled to consider the deaths of George Brewer, Hoke Irving, and three unidentified men, find that the first-named came to his death by gunshot wound inflicted by one Roger

Duval in an unintentional, unavoidable, and ac-
cidental manner connected with the discharge of his
duties as guard in the Esperanza gambling hall,
and that the other four were killed by the same
Roger Duval as a lawful and necessary measure to
prevent murder, larceny, and other crimes the de-
ceased had conspired, intended, and attempted to
commit on the said premises which Duval was hired
to guard."

"Do you order the said Duval held?"

"We do not."

"Release your prisoner."

The deputy gave me a clap on the back, and right
away the place went into the craziest hullabaloo
you ever heard. They yelled for me, stomped on
the floor, shook my hand, and hollered at the bartenders to give me a drink. I didn't want any drink.
I wanted to be alone. But they wouldn't have it
that way, and I had to stand there at the bar pretending to believe I was a hero. And then all of a
sudden you could hear a pin drop. The men from
Brewer's mine had picked him up and were carrying him out when Raymond Brewer must have said
something, because the Marshal called him over.

"Mr. Brewer, say that over again and to me, what you just now said to your men, about the jury's verdict on your brother."

"I said it's a disgrace."

"And how is it a disgrace?"

"Roger Duval meant to kill my brother, that's how."

"You mean—he *murdered* him?"

"He saw his chance when this thing started tonight, and I say it's shameful that he be exonerated, and treated like a public hero, instead of being held for trial like the rat that he is."

"Mister, this is a serious charge."

"You think I don't know it?"

"You got any proof?"

"The idea that Roger Duval could kill somebody by accident is just about as silly as the idea he wouldn't kill him if he had a reason. He's the best gunman in town, he's here because he's a dead shot, and he doesn't hit what he aims to miss, and he doesn't miss what he aims to hit."

"That just says he done it because he done it."

"He did."

"What might this here reason be?"

160

"A woman."

"Just that?"

"Isn't it enough?"

"A man kills a woman over a man, and a woman kills a man over a woman, but a man kills a man over a woman so seldom that I'd have to know a little more about it if I really meant to believe it. Can you tell me who this woman is, and why one man would kill another on account of her?"

"Yeah, she's a—"

I don't know if my hand twitched, or if one of his men gave him a sign, or what. The deputy had let me clean and reload the gun while the inquest was going on, and it was in its regular place under my arm. Anyway, he cut it off in the middle of a snarl, and finished off with: "—a resident of this town."

"That don't prove nothing to me."

"It does to me."

He started out after the body, but every two or three steps he'd turn and look at me and lick his lips, and from the way the whole crowd looked at the both of us, I knew I had that man to kill or he'd do the same for me.

11

When they'd been hollering for me as a hero I
didn't want any drink, but now they were staring at
me as a killer I had to have it. Because maybe
nothing could be proved, but they knew from the
way it was said and the way it was heard that what
had been said was true. And even if it meant nothing to them, except one more thing to bet on, as
which man would get it when the shooting began, it
did to me. I hadn't got used to it, this Western idea
that a man's life was the cheapest thing there was,
and I had killed a man that had never done anything to me but take off my hands the worst girl in
the world for me to have, and I'd shot him in the
back of the head without even giving him a chance
to turn around. Eyes were looking at me, and my

face felt like it was hanging off my cheekbones in pouches. I ordered wheat, because it gets there quicker than rye, and I guess I had a dozen slugs. Then I must have looked queer, because Rocco came over and said take the rest of the night off, so I went home. But I didn't sleep. I lay there, and it got light, and the bugle sounded, and the flag went up on Mount Davidson, and still I lay there, staring out at the sky. I tried to think of Raymond Brewer, and what I had to do to him, and I couldn't. I couldn't take any interest in him, or what I was going to do next, or Morina, or anything. It was like I had turned numb all over.

I must have dropped off, though, because when the knock came I jumped and gave some kind of a moan. It was Mrs. Finn, to tell me a Mr. Arthur Haines was in the front parlor, waiting to see me. I washed up, strapped on my gun, and dressed. When I went in there he had on a new checked suit, and got up and shook hands, though until then he had never shown any great interest in me. He was a good-looking Irishman, in a flashy kind of way, with round, pale face, and light blue eyes that were warm and soft and friendly, specially when he was singing a song, and he picked some girl out there to smile at. I asked him how everything was, and he said fine, and then I asked how he'd like to step out and have a cup of coffee with me, but he said he was due at the International in a few minutes for lunch and wouldn't have time.

"Well, Art, what's on your mind."

"Just a friendly warning, Roger."

"Is any warning friendly?"

"This one's supposed to be."

"What's it about?"

"Renny. And Biloxi. Both of them."

"They're friends of mine."

"They were."

"Well, Art, say it."

"On account of Brewer, they're sore at you, Roger. They were close to him, you know. And then another thing, now he's gone, it's mixed up the house question the worst way. He gave it to her, you know. He gave Biloxi the house, and had it built so there'd be a wonderful music room for Renny, and had all that furniture sent up, some of it from San Francisco, so it's still on the wagons and hasn't been unloaded yet—but not one deed,

164

check, or draft has been signed yet, and Biloxi's going crazy. She's sold out on D Street, and she's lost out on A Street, and Renny's out to get you."

"Why me?"

"The brother says you killed George."

"The brother's a goddam fool."

"And Renny says you did."

"Was he there?"

"He claims he didn't have to be."

"And what have you got to do with it?"

"Roger, it's just like I said. It's a friendly warning, that's all. He says he'll get you, and I don't know if he will or not, but he might try. I'm a good hombre. I don't like to see nice people in trouble."

"Meaning me?"

"And him. And her. All of you."

He lit a cigar, sat back, gave a nod, and that little smile. I tried to get my mind on Renny, but it was like the night before, when I had tried to get my mind on Raymond Brewer and what I was going to do about him, and all I could think about was nothing. But this little smile was going all the time, and all of a sudden it struck me there was something funny about it. What was he doing here, talking to me? I didn't mean a thing to him, and if he was just somebody that knew something, why didn't he get on a stage for Carson or Utah or some place like that and get as far away from it as he could? And if he was such a friend of Renny's, why was he telling me, and giving me the one thing I would need to take care of myself, which was a tip in advance? "Upsets me about Biloxi."

"I can understand that, Roger. She's nice."

"Good-looking, too."

"Yeah, those Creoles have got something."

"How is she?"

"How do you mean, how is she?"

"In bed."

"Good God, Roger, how would I know?"

"She's got it for sale. Haven't you bought any?"

"Roger, you're quite mistaken. Sure, Biloxi's in business. All her life she's been in business, it's the only thing she knows. But since Renny moved in, down in San Francisco after she went there in '52, she's been strictly one man's woman. That was nice, that was. He showed up one night, with a message from her sister, that lives up in Shreveport. He's a little younger than she is, you know, and at that time he was nothing but a nineteen-year-old kid. And he just moved in. I mean, just like that. He took one look at Biloxi, and a few minutes later, when she started upstairs with a colonel from the Presidio, he pulled a rapier out of his walking-stick and said there'd be nothing like that. Biloxi, of course, she loved it, and when she heard him play, that clinched it. No, don't jump to conclusions, Roger. I'm just a friend."

"But you *could* be more?"

"In what way?"

"If Renny got it."

I didn't expect him to jump out of his skin, or do anything, as a matter of fact, except what he did do, which was to act hurt, and smug, and tell me I'd hung around too many gambling saloons to know what real friendship was like. Just the same, for one second he was caught by surprise, and there came this little flicker in his eye, so I knew I wasn't talking so foolish as he said. I thanked him for his warning, and he left. On my way back from breakfast I stopped at a bar and got a pint of wheat.

I don't really like liquor, but all afternoon I lay in bed and drank, trying to get up some interest in what was going to happen to me, and by six o'clock I had a bellyful of booze, but I didn't any more give a damn than I had before. I shaved and washed up, and walked over to the International for dinner. As I walked through the bar it fell quiet as a church, and in the dining room I don't think there was one person that wasn't watching me as I went to my table. There was something about the way they acted that told me things were going on that I didn't know about, and still it seemed to me my whole insides were made of lead. I was due for work at eight, and at a quarter of I stopped in the lobby for a cigar, then started down the street.

As I turned the corner of C for the Esperanza I noticed men standing all up and down the board-walk on the other side, like they were waiting for something. Then, on my side, I noticed not one human being was in sight. I had the boardwalk to myself as far as the Esperanza, but in front of that Raymond Brewer was walking, with Red Caskie beside him, and two other men following behind.

I stopped. From things being said on the other side I knew they had spotted me. I don't know if I felt scared, or how I felt. Since killing that man I hadn't felt anything, except some horrible sense of guilt, and for the rest of it just this vacant pain. I stood there, trying to make myself go on. My feet wouldn't move. I turned around, started back to Union. "Well, that yellow son of a bitch."

I climbed up Union to B and walked home. But when I felt in my pocket for my key, a rifle shot popped down the street and raw splinters jumped out of the front door, where it was lit up by the gaslight on the corner. I drew and turned as quick as anybody ever did, but there was nothing there but brick. I looked at every doorway and window, but couldn't see anything. I went inside and clumped up the long board tunnel to the floor where the rooms started. Mrs. Finn came out of the front parlor. "What was the shooting, Roger?"

"I couldn't see."

"Was it intended for you?"

"It might have been. Your door got ventilated."

"Don't you think it would be safer for you—just so they can't keep track so easy where you are—if you moved somewhere else?"

"No I don't."

"I'll have to have more for your room."

"How much more?"

"Instead of six dollars I want ten."

"All right."

I went in the room, lit the lamp, and started to undress. Then I figured the lamp was a little too much of a good thing, if anybody happened to be watching, so I blew it out. Then I felt around in the dark for my pint of wheat, and had the last drink out of it. Then I lay down on the bed. I lay there quite a while, without dressing or undressing, except pretty soon I took off my coat. I tried to be ashamed I had run out on Raymond Brewer, and to be afraid of Renny, if he was the one that had shot at me. I couldn't get up any interest about either one. They didn't seem real and they didn't seem to have anything to do with me. And then all of a sudden I was off that bed like I had shot up on springs and pulling the door shut after me. If it was imagination I didn't know, but it seemed to me I had seen something coming through that window, from the sidewalk. I took a chair from the landing, jammed it against the door, and went down to the street. Mrs. Finn was looking at me from the landing as I went downstairs with no hat, no coat, and no gun. When I started to undress, I had hung it where I had always hung it, on the bedpost, so it was less than a foot from my head. But when I jumped, I didn't have it.

On Taylor Street, up from the Enterprise, was a miners' hangout, and I went in there and ordered beer. But from the way they acted when I came in, I knew some of them had been in the crowd in front of the Esperanza, and when a couple of them went out, it was no trouble to figure what they were up to, and that wasn't so good. Because by then I had figured out pretty well why I had been acting like I had, which was a pretty funny way to act when you stop to think about it, because up to then I had faced a few slugs, and while I own up I was just as scared as anybody, I claim I wasn't a hell of a sight scareder. The thing was, Brewer meant

171

nothing to me, and Renny didn't, and Biloxi didn't.
But Morina did, and no matter who hollered I was
yellow, I had to face her, and tell her what I had
done, and why I had done it. And yet she was on
her way to San Francisco, and couldn't get back for
a week, and here I'd got myself in a hole where if
I didn't do something pretty quick I wouldn't even
live through the night.

The sergeant came in, the one that had talked
to Brewer and got called down for forgetting that
getting rich for your country is more important
than fighting for it. He gave the miners the old
recruiting spiel, about how wonderful the army
grub is, and how the new uniforms have just come
in, and how good-looking they are. He let them feel
of the one he was wearing, to see what fine wool it
is. And then I thought of the United States Govern-
ment, and how it doesn't let its soldiers get killed
until the proper time comes. "Well, Bud, where do
you take these rookies of yours, after you get
them?"

"First we bed them down in our recruiting office

in Gold Hill, in a back room we got, then when we get a bunch we take them to San Francisco."

"That back room, is it under guard?"

"That's not for a soldier to worry about."

"I want to know."

"There's a sentry out there."

"Then let's go."

And an hour later, when I sat on the edge of a bunk with the stuff they'd given me, I knew I was as low as I could get, that I would put this uniform on, instead of the one that was mine, for the sake of one more look at something that had brought me nothing but misery since I'd seen her. And next day, when Raymond Brewer saw me with a squad in dungarees, and laughed at me, and I did nothing about it, for the first time in my life I felt yellow.

"Duval?"

"Yo."

"Visitor."

She was out there in the dark, still in her travelling dress. I could feel a drawstring tighten around my stomach as I went over to her, because I knew my piece by heart, but I didn't know what hers was, or whether it was engraved on a bullet. But when I got to her, it looked like there were two drawstrings out there, the tightest one around her face. It was all twisted, like she was in pain, and it was hard to remember she'd ever been pretty. She took hold of me and looked in my eyes, like she was trying to see in them something she had to find out about. It was quite some time before she spoke, and when she did it was in a whisper. "You did it, didn't you, Roger?"

"Who do you think did it?"

"I know it was you, but tell me."

"I killed that bastard, I meant to kill him, and I'll kill any other bastard you sell yourself to, and if there's just one more bastard I'll kill you."

"Kiss me, Roger."

". . . What?"

"I never knew there was any such feeling as this."

"The only feeling you get is from money."

"Not like this. That you'd kill him. For me."

I held her tight and kissed her, and she didn't kiss like she had in Sacramento, when she always

174

seemed to be laughing at me, but in a hot, hungry way, with tears in her eyes. "I can't pass this night without you, Roger."

"Listen, this is a men-only army."

"Then you'll have to leave it."

"God, do I want to!"

"Where'll we go?"

"I guess not to Biloxi's."

"Oh Roger, the most awful thing happened. They set her out in the street. And the piano broke down the boardwalk and went sliding down into a yard back of one of the houses on B Street. And Renny tried to stop it, and it mashed him, and he's hurt. Biloxi moved him to Arthur Haines's."

"Arthur'll take care of him."

"You think so?"

"I know it."

"But where can we go, Roger?"

"I know an old mine."

"All right."

"It's no International Hotel."

"I won't mind."

So how I left the U. S. Army was walk off and leave it, her hand pressed in mine, take an omnibus

to Virginia, pick up my blankets and clothes that
had been sent to Mrs. Finn's, get my gun again, and
then take her to Pioneer for her stuff that was
checked there. Then we climbed the mountain. We
went up to an old drift Paddy and I had run across
when we were all over the place organizing the
union. We cut piñon branches with my jack-knife,
and laid them in the tunnel mouth, and on top of
them made our bed. We didn't make very quick
work of it, on account of being in each other's arms
all the time, and I don't know which was most exciting, tearing that uniform off at last, or tearing
off her clothes. Except that the little black dress
didn't seem to need much tearing. She was wrig-
gling out of it and into the blankets even before I
took hold of it, and when she slipped into my arms,
all naked and warm, she closed her eyes before she
kissed me, and her face looked like she was in
church.

"Roger, this never happened to me."

"To me either."

"Nothing like it. Ever."

"Do you know when I knew you were mine?"

"When, Roger?"

"That night, under the pier."

"That was sweet. . . . *Roger!*"

She raised on one elbow and looked down on me with eyes so big they frightened me. ". . . What is it, Morina?"

"I never been had by a man before!"

"You really mean that, don't you?"

"Of course! It's the first time!"

And so in Brewer's blood we washed out all she had been, and said we were married, and that she was a virgin until this night, and that I was.

We stayed there two days. We both had a little money, and she'd drop down in the town and buy stuff and carry it to the mouth of the gully, and I'd meet her and carry it the steep part of the path, and then I'd tie a string to the basket handle and she'd climb the ladder that led to our drift mouth and pull it up. In the mine a little way was a spring of the cold water they generally struck at the upper levels, and in a toolbox I found an old lunch bucket, so we were all right for something to boil in. For firewood I used mine timbers that I broke up with a pickaxe that was in the box. Late the first day, in the brush, I spotted some quail and got two before they rose. Broiled, with an old mine needle run through them for a spit, they were pretty good. The second day, while she was down in the town, I looked up from the paper she had brought the day before, and in front of me, coming across the ledge, was a young goat, what they call a kid. In Virginia there's no grazing for cows, but goats can make out, and a few people keep them, for the milk they give, and to eat. I got out my gun, and laughed at how I'd clean my visitor and skin him before she got back, tell her it was a lamb that must have strayed from some butcher's yard, and then have a joke on her after she'd eaten a few slices. But then I thought: How the hell did he get here? We used a ladder, but he couldn't, even if he was a goat. And there wasn't any other way up there, that I knew of.

He kept coming and I kept quiet, where I was sitting at the head of the ladder, so I could watch the mouth of the gully. When he saw me he stopped, but after he thought it over he came on again and turned into the drift. The blankets and stuff slowed him down too, but pretty soon he went in. I tiptoed over and peeped. The water was what he wanted, and as soon as he sucked up a bellyful he came out, looked me over again, and started back. I followed, and he ran. And then he just wasn't there. It was like some trick on a stage, where the fellow waves a tablecloth and the rabbit is gone. I went over to the last place he was, and all I could see was **a** straight face of rock. But then I happened to step to one side, and all of a sudden, from that angle, you could see a hole, kind of a crack, about four feet high, and ten or twelve inches across at its widest place, which was at the bottom. I lay on my belly and looked. As far as you could really see, the crack went straight into the rock, but further inside there was some sort of a reflection that looked like there was an opening. I got some candles from the toolchest, lit one, and crawled in.

The crack, I suppose, kept on for twenty or thirty feet, but then it led into an old stope, one of those rooms they kept working on until it's as big as a three-story house. This was that big at least, but the weight of the top had crushed the timbering, so everything had caved in, and probably opened the crack I had come in by. But when I worked past the rubble my heart almost stopped beating at what was dead ahead of me, part of the

raw rock that had been uncovered by the fall of
the top. It was ore, and while I couldn't tell and
nobody could tell, until the assayers got busy, if
it would run $3,000 to the ton or $300 to the ton,
anybody could tell it was sulphuret of silver, a
beautiful blue-black, as nice a strike as had been
made on the lode since Comstock sold out for $11,-
000. I climbed over on a fallen twelve-by and dug
a piece out with my knife. It was soft, and crum-
bled in my fingers. It was wonderful, just to touch
it.

Somewhere a pebble fell, and I remembered my
little goat. I had to know how he got here, because
if I had followed him in, anybody could. I put
out my candle and waited. After a long time, a half
hour maybe, my eyes got used to the dark so it
wasn't quite black any more. Then, opposite the
crack I had come in by, I saw where the light was
coming from. It was the upper part of an entry, the
bottom all blocked by rock. I got over there and
looked. A few feet inside was a winz that dipped
down to a drift mouth on the other side of the hill,
and that explained it. When animals go in a mine,
they're generally looking for salt, and that's what

181

had probably brought my friend in. But I kicked down enough rock to block that entry altogether, so he couldn't come back.

"I won't give it up, Roger, all that beautiful money."

"We'll have to, until after the war."

"Why do we have to? All you do is take an option. On an old run-down mine like this, that's been abandoned for years, they'd think they were lucky to get a hundred dollars for a thirty-day look-see. Then when your papers are signed you uncover your *bonanza*, and you can get all the money you need to start mining, from the bank. It's done every day."

"I'm talking about the army."

"They let you buy your way out."

"Either that or they shoot you."

"They never do that."

"They almost never do it. It's only occasionally they do it, when it's necessary to make an example of somebody to remind all soldiers that they can do it when they want to, and they will do it if they have to. Unfortunately, I don't know if now is the time they feel they've got to make an example, or just the time when they take a broad-minded attitude."

"We've got to have this money."

"I'm all for it. But how?"

"And now. Somebody else might find it."

"I was even worried about the goat."

"You've got to think of something."

"If we could only buy it."

"You mean now?"

"So it would be waiting for us, after the war."

"How much would it cost?"

"Ten, fifteen thousand, maybe. Maybe less. This outfit that owns it is always in trouble, and especially lately. But a lot more than we've got."

She lay there a long time, and when it began to get light her eyes were still open, staring at the sky outside. Then: "Roger."

"Yes?"

"You know Red Caskie?"

"I guess so."

"You know what he does?"

"He's the Brewer dog-robber, isn't he?"

"He does all kinds of things, but mainly he makes one trip a month down to San Francisco. You know what that trip's for?"

". . . I can guess."

"Yes, it's for gold. The silver goes down on the stages, by Wells, Fargo, every day, and nobody bothers it because it's heavy and not a great deal goes by any single coach. But once a month the mint pays for the bullion in gold, and Will Brewer stays down there to take care of that and whatever other business the company has. And then Caskie brings it back."

"When does he go?"

"Never the same day of the month, never the same boat down to San Francisco, never the same coach line, always a little bit different, so nobody can be waiting for him along the line."

"How much does he bring?"

"How much do they send down?"

"In silver, they're running a thousand a day."

"Thirty thousand a month?"

"Around that."

"Then that's what he brings back." She stretched, yawned, and snuggled into my arms. "So then,

184

after we get it, I'll slip up here with it, and buy this mine, and when the war's over we can have anything we want."

"Wait a minute, not so fast."

Because sitting here, reading what I've just written, all I can see is two people fixing to commit a crime. But then, especially after that week I spent in the Union army, it seemed like I had to do something that was some good to my country, and that this could be it. I mean, if $30,000 in gold was coming from California, to pay men to dig $30,000 in silver, to pay men to shoot my people, and I could get it, it looked like the right thing to do. I wanted her to get that part straight, and I was solemn as hell while I was explaining it to her. But all she did was pull me closer, and kiss all around my mouth, and into my mouth.

The old shack, across the river from Sacramento, was exactly as I had left it, even to the rowboat back of the pump, where I had dragged it so it would be out of sight, and after we had aired the rooms out it hardly seemed we had been away. I had rented it from a fellow named Mouton that had the farm along that part of the river, but instead of walking over there and telling him I was back I decided to lay low for the few days we'd be around, and tell him nothing. If he hadn't even bothered to unlock it and get it ready for the next fellow, it didn't look like he got over there very often, and it might be that he kept track of those dodgers over at the postoffice that told about the men wanted by the army, and had spotted my name. Every morning I'd stroll over the bridge and buy a glass of beer across the street from the Sacramento Valley Railroad, which anybody would have to use coming from Virginia City, unless he was going to put himself to an awful lot of trouble, no matter how he mixed up his steamboats and stagecoach lines. It ran as far as Folsom, and it was there that the coaches started. And sure enough, one day in October, here came Caskie. He had a bag, and he stayed on the train to Front and K Streets, and went aboard the Yosemite. It left at six, so when he came off a little later without any luggage, that just meant he was passing the time in town, so I went on across the river.

_186_

"When's he due back, and how?"

"Well, that ought to be easy, Roger."

"Will you tell me what's easy about it?"

"Well, can't we watch some more?"

"Which line do we watch? There are six boats he can come by, all leaving San Francisco the same time, and all getting here within a few minutes of each other. Which hotel does he stop at? We can't go around asking for him, or looking at the registers, because he knows us both, and that's all he needs to know, that we've been snooping after him. How do we know he goes to a hotel? Maybe he goes direct from the boat to the train, like he went from the train to the boat, and he's here and gone before we've even got started on what we're going to do about him."

"There has to be some way."

"There doesn't have to be anything."

We talked about it all afternoon and half the night, and the more we talked, the clearer it became to me that the only part of his trip we could be certain about was the train ride from San Francisco to Folsom, and if there was some way I could go on ahead and find out in advance when he had

187

started, then we might be able to do what we figured to do with some chance of getting away with it. In the middle of the night I woke her up. "Come on, let's pack."

"What, *now?*"

"In the morning we leave."

"Where are we going?"

"Folsom."

We got to Folsom around seven thirty, let a hotel hack take our stuff over the river to the town, and then stood around to watch how they did, transferring passengers and express to twenty or thirty stages that were pulled up there. It was like I remembered it, from my first trip up there. The runners were all over the platform beating up business for whatever line they worked for. As fast as the passengers would make up their mind, the runner would take his luggage over and stow it in the luggage carrier on back of the coach. But the messengers, they weren't paying attention to luggage or stuff like that. They were up front, at the baggage car, with the Wells, Fargo man, checking

188

it over what they were responsible for, and some
of it was regular packages coming up the line, or
maybe around from the East by boat and up, but
after they had been transferred they got down to
the real thing, which was the metal boxes to be
transferred, some to one coach, some to another.
They held money, and the messengers split it up
which one was to stand by while the Wells, Fargo
man helped the others carry them to whichever
coach they were consigned to. But on those boxes
there was no way to tell if they held $5 or $500 or
$5,000, or were coming back empty. The mes-
sengers, they rode guard on all boxes.

I held my watch, to see how long it took, and the
first coach didn't pull out till a half hour after the
train got in. We walked over to the town to find a
spot she could stand on and watch what Caskie did,
once he got off the train. That wasn't easy, because
for stuff like that you think of a saloon, but at that
hour of day a girl pretending to take a drink and
watching a railroad station would attract attention,
and in that country just to start somebody wondering what you're up to is to get in trouble, because
they don't generally figure out that you're up to

189

something good. And besides, the saloons didn't
give a good view. At Folsom there's the American
River, with the town on one side, the railroad on
the other, and a bridge in between, but half the
saloons got their back to the river, and they block
the view from the ones that face it, so that idea
looked pretty sick from the start. We had walked
clear down to the stables on the west end, where
the old town was, when I hit on what we needed, or
thought I had. We came back to the hotel, and I
said: "I have business up the line, but my wife is
staying, and I want her to be comfortable, in a nice
room. Can we have one up high, in front?"

"I can give you third floor, a beautiful bright
room overlooking the river, with unobstructed view
of the valley—"

"That's fine."

"Of course the rate's a little higher—"

"How much?"

"For your wife, four dollars."

"That's all right, but I want to see it."

"I'll take you up myself."

If I had built it special it couldn't have been
better. It looked right down on the station, so she

could see everything that went on down there, and if she raised the window, she could even hear what was said. "Now remember, after you spot him you check out and send your baggage over. Then you tell the porter you forgot something, come up here—"

"They'll have the key, though. At the desk."

"That's right. You've checked out. Let's see—"

"Couldn't I leave the door open?"

"Right. Come in here, watch Caskie—"

"Spot the coach he's traveling on—"

"Have your wires ready."

"I go running over to the station, hail the driver of Caskie's coach, have my things put aboard, go into the station and file my wire, the one that says meet me."

"And if he doesn't come tomorrow—"

"File the other one, that I'll be a day late."

"Wear the white hat, but if anything comes up that looks suspicious, or that causes us to call it off, take off the hat and put on the red coat."

"When Caskie sees me—"

"Say hello and act natural."

"Hold me tight, Roger. I'm so excited."

The local stage I had to take to Placerville was
slow and I didn't get there till three o'clock in the
afternoon. I went to the Pioneer stables and bought
me a couple of horses with money she had given
me, with bridles and Mexican saddles, for easy
riding. I left one there, got on the other one, and
rode back the way I had come, so I could use the
last hour of daylight to check up things I had to
know. Placerville is in the first of the foothills,
and below the town is rising ground, where anything pulled by horses has to slow down to a walk.
I put the horse up the bank and skirted the edge of
the woods at a walk, until pretty soon I found what
I wanted. It was a bend, where I could stay in the
trees, yet at the same time have a view of the road,
not only what was coming up but what was going
down. Then I rode into the woods a way, and found
out there was no timber-cutting, charcoal-burning,
or anything like that going on, though here and
there were places where they had been doing
plenty, and not so long ago. But right now anybody
in those woods pretty much had it to himself. I
rode on up in the hills a mile or so, and saw there
was clear passage over to the river without having

to follow any trail where people were likely to be. Then I rode right down to the river and saw there was pretty good footing along the bank, but by that time it was dark. I rode back, had some dinner at a chuck wagon, then went to bed.

Next morning, after I had something to eat and went back to the hotel, waiting around for that wire was an awful long time. I had given the telegrapher at Wells, Fargo the name of Bob Davis, which I was using at the hotel, and which she was to use when she wired me, and told him if anything came in I'd be over to pick it up. Finally, when it was time to go over there, he was just copying it down when I came in the door, and it said: "Sorry darling unable to make it today better luck tomorrow." I went out and had a drink. When I walked back to my room my legs felt light. When the liquor wore off I wanted more. And then I knew why I felt like that. I was glad it was called off, even if it was for only a day.

I did some more riding around in the afternoon, partly to get a better line on the upper stretches of the river, partly to get acquainted with both horses. They weren't either one of them really good, but they weren't so bad either. They were Western mustangs, small but tough, and why I wanted them for what we had to do was they could probably get along on light rations, and, if they had to, forage up what they needed at night. That was one reason I was following the river. At least, somewhere along the way, there'd be grass and some kind of life I could shoot, or catch in the water, or something.

Before eating that night, I had the stable put me up four sacks of oats, ten pounds apiece. I wanted more, but kept remembering the weight of the gold that had to go on those saddles along with us. I weigh a hundred and eighty, and even if I put all the gold on her horse, we'd be traveling awful heavy. And yet I had to have something for the horses to eat. No way to feed rabbits to them.

"Leaving now by Pioneer dying to see you Josie." I had about an hour. I went to the stable,

194

saddled up, paid my bill. They had done like I said, fixed up the oats so they'd ride back of the saddle, and given me a halter to lead with. I started out. On the streets people turned to look at me, though a rider leading another horse was about the commonest thing you could see at that time in the West. Or maybe I just thought they were looking. The horse I was on acted all right, but the other one didn't want to be led, and he kept hanging back and fighting me. And then when I came to the hill, and the spot where I wanted to go into the woods, my horse would go up the bank and the other one wouldn't. It took me ten minutes, getting off and fighting them both, to get them up, and another five minutes to get them both quiet. Going through the woods it was worse, because the second horse would take a dive on the other side of some bush, and I'd have to wheel and back up to get him clear. I meant to tie them both up to trees, but I couldn't have them too near the road. They might nicker, for one thing, and I had to have room to make a quick dash after we got the money.

At last I was at the bend, and behind a tree, with my red bandanna handkerchief ready to slip over my face, but my heart almost went through my heels when I looked at that road. It was crawling with traffic. I don't think I ever saw so many freight wagons, not only loaded ones going up, but empty ones coming back, and not only wagons, but long strings of mules, where they could pull the empty wagons back with six and eight, and saved brakemen if they sent the mules on down in strings. And just to make things worse, a fellow showed up with a snatch team wearing the tassels of Pioneer, and it was easy to see he was there for the day. Unless it just happened that he and his six mules were at the bottom of the hill hooking on to a wagon, or up at the top, casting loose, he'd be in the way all the time. I began to feel cold in the feet. And then, down the road, I saw a spot of red. It got nearer, and sure enough it was an Overland coach, coming along behind six grays, and she was on top, with no hat and the red coat that was to be the danger signal. I could slip off through the woods, get my horses, and ride back to town without having to throw down on anybody at all. I was so happy I could sing.

"Roger, did I do wrong to get scared?"

"You got to think fast and decide."

"I did everything, exactly as you told me, and it seemed funny that it was all coming out the way you said it would, from the porter getting worried I would miss the coach, to the driver doing all he could to accommodate a girl that was asking a favor, to the old telegraph operator that had jokes about how anxious I was to see my husband. And all that time I hadn't run into Caskie. But when I came out of the station to climb up to the top, he jumped out of the coach, where he had already gone aboard, and looked at me without speaking, and then told the driver to go back to the company office. They looked like they thought he was crazy, but they did what he said and he went in there. When he came out he had two more guards, with rifles, and they climbed up behind me and I didn't know what to do. But that meant three rifles up there, and I thought it was too many. I took off the hat and put on the red coat, and—did I do wrong, darling?"

We had got to Placerville almost the same time, and she was in front of the Cary House coming off the coach when I got there with my two horses. We lay down after lunch and she started to talk, and I listened like I was a brave hombre that was a little disappointed but would forgive because I really had a big heart. But her eyes were so black, and she looked at me so serious, that pretty soon I had to laugh. She laughed too. "If you love me I'll tell you something."

"I've always loved you, Roger."

"I was scared too."

"But you'd have done it."

"I'm not so sure."

"I am."

"Then I'd have made a mess of it."

"I wish I'd worn the hat. I could have cried when I saw that coach drive on, with him in it and all that gold, that lovely money."

"I laughed, I was so happy."

That night we lay close, but we didn't have much to say. On her end of it, she had lost the money and the chance to get hold of the mine, and I guess I cared about that part, too. But mostly I hated it that I wasn't doing anything for my country at all. If I was grabbing gold that the North needed, all right I was a hero. But if I wasn't, I was nothing but a gunman laying up with a girl, and not much of a gunman at that, because I hadn't even done what I figured to do. She began running over it again, how it had all happened: "It was all so wonderful. There he was, stepping out of the baggage car with the Wells, Fargo man, and in a minute there went the money over, and I knew which coach it was, and—"

"Out of the—*which* car, did you say?"

"The baggage car. Where they had the money."

"Not a passenger car?"

"No, the front car."

I thought and I thought, and then I really told her how crazy we had been to think we could do it the way I had laid it out. In the first place, we were right on top of it and we still had no way to carry the stuff, even if we got it. In the second place, we were foolish enough to think we could face armed men that were always expecting trouble, and get away with it. In the third place and the worst place, we had made no provision for a real

199

getaway, beyond riding up a river we had never seen, headed for what we called the "cattle country," with no idea how we were going to get out of it once we were in it, or with anything worked out better than faith, hope, and guesswork. "Go on, Roger, I'm listening."

"We're getting that money. Next trip."

"But how?"

"We're stealing that train."

"But the people—"

"Won't stop us for one second."

"Oh if we only could!"

"And the key to the whole thing, the getaway, we make a real one. That's the trouble with these punks out here, these fools that think they're bad men. They don't know how to shoot, and they don't know any geography, so they can start some place and have some kind of a chance of getting there. But me, I do. I studied it all the time I was sending those dispatches, I know how the land lays and I know every little thing that goes on. You know how we're getting out of here?"

"Tell me."

"Mexico."

"But we can't get there!"

"Why not?"

"Either we have to head south and travel over all the southern part of the state, where there'll certainly be word about us, or we've got to go back to San Francisco, and that's terribly dangerous, or —but *how?*"

"The Colorado River."

". . . Where's that?"

"Not too far away. We grab that gold just a little the other side of Folsom, and we light out toward Sonora. Then we hit the Stanislaus River and go up over the pass to the Owens River country and go down to the lake. No trouble so far. Game, water, grass for the horses, everything we need. Then we got it bad a few days because we've got to cross the Mojave Desert. But probably that's really good, because there's hardly any communication across that part of the country, and nobody'll be looking for us, or know who we are. Then we hit Callville and a steamer."

"For where?"

"Port Isabel."

"I never even heard of it."

"It's there. Then the C. S. A. Later, our silver mine."

"Oh, it's wonderful!"

13

Three days later we were back in the shack on the Yolo side of the Sacramento River, but I think we learned more in that time than either of us had ever learned in any other three days of our life. We sent her trunks down by express, and then I made her ride back to Sacramento with me just the way she'd have to ride for the Colorado, in a man's dungarees, with man's boots, hat, and shirt, and we got them all in Placerville for her, in boy's sizes, fairly cheap. She could ride a man's saddle all right, because she'd ridden that way in Venezuela, except she had a riding mule there, and held the reins out wide in each hand, besides cocking her feet up front in a short stirrup, so she looked funny but rode fairly easy. But what we ran into, that first night out of Placerville, almost made your blood run cold when you stopped to think it would have been our second night in the open if we'd gone ahead with what we had started to do, and no way to have done anything about it. To begin with, it rained. And then we woke up that we had nothing against rain except blankets, and no food or things to cook food in, or anything to drink. The horses ate, and I watered them in the river. But we went hungry, and lay on the wet ground, and shivered. She wanted to go to one of those teamster places for the night, but I was bullheaded. If this was what we'd elected ourself to, we might as well get started on it, and if there was plenty we had to learn, we'd better learn it now than later. We were a sick-looking pair when we trotted into Folsom, but we knew what we had to buy. The first thing we got was two oilcloth pack covers, that we could lay on if that was all we needed, but could put up for a tent if we ran into nights like last night. Then we got a skillet. It's the California tool, and they got jokes all over the place about it, and yet we'd forgotten it. Then we got canteens. Then we got

204

bacon, flour, sugar, salt, and beans. Then we had
something to eat, and felt better.

The second night, coming from Folsom into
Sacramento, we found out we didn't really know
anything about horses. My family had had a horse
in Annapolis, and I had taken care of him a good
bit of the time, but watering and feeding and bed-
ding a horse in your own backyard is one thing,
and watering and tethering and feeding him on a
long ride is completely different. You got to figure
how much feed he needs, that you've got to carry,
how much he can do for himself on the pasture you
find for him, how much line he's got to have, how
far you can ride him in a day, a whole lot of things
that don't come up with a horse and carriage
around a nice little town like Annapolis, with
brick houses and nice green lawns. We worked and
cussed and watched and got acquainted with our
animals and finally began to get it down better,
so it was easier. I learned one thing too I was to
use several times later.

The night we left Folsom we pitched by the river,
I staked out the horses, found wood for a fire, then

went looking for a rabbit. So of course, when what you need is a rabbit, all you see is a crow. But then, from a boulder over the river, I happened to notice a pool, and down in it were fish. I could see them, where they'd flash silver in the sun. And once more I began to cuss, because of course that was one more thing we forgot, a hook and line. But I climbed down there with my gun and stuck it in the water. I was pretty nervous, because I couldn't remember if that made it explode, or what it did. It pretty near jerked my arm out of the socket, but that was all. In a minute, floating all around, were my fish, and I hooked them out with a stick and went running back to where she was frying bacon over the fire. So instead of bacon and beans we had fried trout and greens that she found, with strips of fried bacon. We weren't really good yet, but we were getting a whole lot better.

After we got two or three things straightened out, like a shed for the horses, and her riding over to Mouton and paying him some rent under the name of Davis, and a book started, to write down all those things we needed but would forget if we didn't make a note of them, I went over and got started on my main job for the next two weeks. I mean I got myself hired on, firing the George F. Bragg, which was the freight engine of the Sacramento Valley Railroad. Because the one thing I had to know before anything else was how to handle a locomotive, and it wasn't something you could pick up by peeping through a spy glass while the cars went down Front Street. I had to be able to do whatever I had to do, and it was tough the way I had to learn it. The engineer was Cap Nixon, and he thought he was the onriest, crustiest article, next to a gator man, that had been seen up to then, and he was crazy on the subject of the goddam firemen being no good. So for the first few days I rolled the sweat and he cussed me out. And then he decided I was an exception, a young fellow that really wanted to learn, and began teaching me. He didn't only show me every gauge and petcock and reverse bar in his cab, but he gave me all the fine points on how to make the run to Folsom, how to slow down for the curves and twists, how to pick up time on the straight stretches, and all the rest of

it. It bothered me, at Folsom, when we'd pull away
for the transfer to the Sacramento, Placer & Nevada, for the run up to Auburn, because they made
kind of a railroad man's convention out of it, with
everybody on both lines cussing each other out one
minute and passing the time of day the next. I
didn't want to get acquainted, because the more of
them that knew me, the worse it was for what I
was up to. I might have to throw down on men that
knew me, no matter how many bandannas I wore.
So when the shifting would go on, I'd take that
time to shine up the Bragg, and get her brass
nice and bright, and bring out her colors. So of
course Cap he loved that. He began spreading it
around that at last he had a fireman, and by God
he was going to make an engineman out of him,
too.

"I heard something today, Roger. About
Caskie."

"Yes, what was it?"

"He has a girl. In San Francisco."

"Ah, that's important!"

"I thought so. Because it looks like, whenever he goes down, he'd lay over at least one night, the way he did last time, instead of coming back the same day he got there."

"That's it."

"It makes everything much simpler."

"Where'd you hear this?"

"From a girl I used to know in New Orleans. I ran into her when I went down to buy clothes that time. It was before Biloxi caught me with the wire, and I was telling her—a whole lot of things. And I happened to mention Red. Last time he was down, she met him, and this blonde he's got. Between what he told her and what I did, she decided to try her luck in Nevada."

"Now we can really line things up."

While I was firing the Bragg, it seemed like the first of the month would never come, and then all of a sudden it was here, and it seemed there wasn't enough time in the day for all we had to do. At last I had sat down with a pencil and paper and figured up the load on my horses. My horse, with

209

me, my saddle, and my pack, would be carrying 225 pounds, at least. I figured the gold at 100 pounds, so her horse, with her saddle and the metal split into two saddle bags, and her pack, would be carrying 225 and over, well over, close to 240. That meant, if we were going to make any time at all, we had to have another horse for feed, rations, and all the other stuff we had to take with us. So with my railroad wages I bought one, with pack saddle. Then, the more I worked it out, the clearer I saw it: however we split it up while we were traveling, she would have to be the one to handle the horses at the time we were doing the job. So all day long I'd make her saddle them, unsaddle them, stake them out, saddle up again, strip them again, get so she could do it in her sleep, and do it quick. Then another thing began to bother me. It was all right, the idea to split the train, and steal that baggage car with the gold and Caskie in it, and leave the coaches behind. But those coaches could roll. They could roll, and as soon as the brakeman, conductor, and passengers found out what had happened, they'd be out on that platform, and how could I tell how soon they'd slacken speed? Half the hombres in California carried guns, and that meant they'd be shooting at her forever before she got far enough ahead to be safe. There was only one thing that would leave us safe. That string of coaches had to be derailed. But how to do it was something I couldn't figure out, and I figured plenty. But at last, just after I quit the fireman job, I had it, or thought I had. I went to the Hopkins store on K Street and bought me a two-foot length of one-inch quarry steel, the eight-sided stuff they use to block-hole with before they put in powder. When I got it home I rigged up a little forge with two bricks and a charcoal fire, and all one Sunday I pounded on it, putting a point on one end and a bulge on the other, what they call upsetting it. Then I laid a broomstick on the ground for the rail, and made her stand on the back stoop and pitch for it. I got it through her head she didn't have to be accurate, didn't have to be good. Anywhere inside the rail was all right, so that steel bar fell across it and laid there half a second till the car wheel hit it. Then I figured something had to bust. She was the one that thought up the idea of carrying it in a basket over her arm.

"Roger, he's here."

"Is he aboard his boat for San Francisco?"

"Yes, the *Chrysopolis*."

Two more days, and we were ready now, and
all we could do was lie there and smoke these
cigarrillos of hers, that I'd got in the habit of in
the last few weeks, and hold each other close, and
sometimes tremble a little. "Morina."

"Yes, Roger?"

"I tell you one thing. If we get away with this,
I'm going in the Confederate Army, and so are
you. That's one way we can prove we mean what
we say we mean."

"What can I do in the army?"

"Whatever they've got."

"How about our mine?"

"It'll have to wait."

"Do you love me?"

"Yes."

"Then all right."

The train ran out R Street, but didn't pick up
speed until it passed Seventeenth. She was to buy

her ticket early, in the station at the foot of K Street, and keep out of sight until his boat was in and he was aboard the baggage car, which was the first car back of the engine, with the gold. Then she was to keep the station between herself and him, and board the front coach, by the rear end. Then she was to walk through it to a seat up front. She had on her same little traveling dress, with poke bonnet, but in the bonnet she had sewed a ruff, so it was hard to see her face. If anything went wrong, like he didn't come after all, she was to go to the front platform at Thirteenth Street, take a sandwich out of the basket, unwrap the newspaper around it and throw that off the train, and eat the sandwich. Then she was to ride to Folsom and come back. But I, where I was posted at Seventeenth, would see the paper and keep off, and next day we'd start over.

But here came the train, coasting along easy with the bell ringing, and no newspaper. I looked around, and nobody was in sight. I stepped out from the Chinese laundry on the corner and walked over to the track. Neither the fireman nor the engineer could see me. The engineer hangs out of his

cab on the right, where all his signals are, and the
fireman doesn't look anywhere but at his woodpile,
as I knew better than anybody else. The locomotive
was the Sacramento, and when it came even with
me I turned and started to trot beside it up the
track. I wasn't so spry with it as I'd been when I
practiced it on the George F. Bragg when Cap
Nixon wasn't looking, as I'd taken the horses up
the day before, and had to foot it back, thirteen
miles of it, early in the morning. But I had speed
enough, and as she pulled ahead and the tender
was going by I sprinted a few feet, caught the
handhold with my left hand, and the rear tender
step with my right foot. That was the hardest thing
I had had to learn, I guess, to reverse the natural
right-handed, left-footed grab when you're boarding the left side of the train. But I had it down
pat by now, and slammed up against the iron exactly right. I held on a few seconds to get steady,
then leaned over to see if I could hear anything in
the baggage car. In the compartment next the
engine was the Wells, Fargo stuff, in the middle
was United States mail, and on the other end was
baggage. The partitions had doors in them, but

they bolted on the side of the mail, and they stayed bolted, if the mail clerk did what he was supposed to do. In Wells, Fargo, if anybody was riding with the messenger, they generally played cards, and that meant they wouldn't be noticing much up front, because they'd be below the level of the little window high up in the end door. I heard somebody count high, low, jack, and game, so that part was like I figured on.

Next, I raised up, to see what was going on in the cab. The train had picked up a little now, and if they ran this locomotive like Cap had run his, she was due for a little wood. But the fireman was just looking at the scenery and wasn't doing anything about wood at all. It came to me, we generally had three times as many cars as this engine was hauling, and probably she didn't need firing quite as quick. And there wasn't a thing I could do, because before I could move, the drop gate had to be up, to screen me. The tender has tanks on the sides and at the back, but in the middle is a narrow place filled with wood stacked crosswise, and to keep it from sliding all over the cab there's a drop gate, an iron plate that runs in grooves between the

215

tanks and that raises with a bar. When you fire, you up with the gate, and I had to have it up, because unless it was, the tips of my fingers, where I'd be sliding along the outside of the tender, could be seen from the cab. And unless it was up, I couldn't be sure the fireman would be stooped over, pitching chunks into his firebox.

I began to get nervous somebody would see me, from out in a field, and I changed my position, so I'd look like one of the train crew that just happened to be riding there, for some reason. I kept peeping, and then began to wonder what I'd do if we overshot the horses and still I couldn't move.

Then all of a sudden I heard a squeak, and it was up. I hooked my fingers over the top of the tender, kept my head down, and slid out on the flange that runs around the bottom of the tender body, like a little catwalk. I had practiced it forty times, and I knew exactly how long it would take me to get to the handhold and the step at the front of the tender, just behind the cab. It would be six seconds. This time, though, it took a little longer. I kept worrying about people seeing me from the field, and stopped two or three times to look around, and that slowed me. So far as I could see, I wasn't seen. It was open country, with nobody around.

When I got my foot on the step and caught the handhold, the fireman was still pitching wood. I had expected to throw down on him, from my coat pocket where I had shifted the gun so I could use it with my left hand, and wigwag him to jump without hollering at the engine driver, because if that hombre threw his reverse bar and shot his steam, I'd be out there in the middle, with a stalled locomotive and five hundred passengers swarming over me and nothing to look forward to but a neck-tie party that wouldn't do Jeff Davis any good at all. But when I started to draw I changed my mind. Because when the fireman finished pitching and kicked shut his firebox door, he did what I'd done a thousand times. He stood there gawping at his gauge, hoping for a little rise. His back was to me and I reached for the back collar of his shirt. I grabbed, jerked, and pitched, and out he went on his head, and didn't move, that I could see, after he hit the dirt. The engineer never noticed a thing, and we kept rolling along, him leaning out of his window, looking straight ahead. I stepped inside, threw down, and touched him on the shoulder. "Jump, pardner, jump."

He rolled down the other bank, and at last I had my train. But before I could even reach for the throttle, which was still on the notch he had given it, or sound the three shorts on the whistle she was waiting for, there came this jerk that threw me up against the tender, the signal gong snapped once, and there went the cord, whistling over the tender and to hell and gone through the eyehole in the baggage car. That was the first thing I figured out wrong. I don't know why, but I had been picturing it that if we cut the train back of the baggage car, that's where the signal cord would part too, and we were ready for what we thought would happen on that basis, because first off we thought all attention, for a minute or two anyway, would be centered behind. But it never occurred to me the cord would break at its weakest point, which of course was the frazzled part next to the gong in the cab. So of course that meant eyes front. So of course that meant Caskie recognizing me where my bandanna slipped off, and opening up without waiting to hear any more.

But that was only the first thing that went wrong. On her end of it, at the wrecked Conestoga wagon she came out on the platform of the first passenger car like she was supposed to, to wait for my whistle signal that would tell her I was cutting the steam so the car would run up and make slack in the coupling, then step across to the baggage car platform, lift the pin, and throw her steel. Then she had things to do with the baggage man when he came running out, if he did. But, like I said, I couldn't take care of my end of it as soon as I had figured on. And that left her standing there. And the baggage man, when he saw a pretty girl out there, came out and started to chin. So she was afraid to be short with him, and that put ideas in his head. He began inviting her in with the baggage, and by now she didn't know what she was going to do about my signal, even if she got it. She had to do something, so she told him she'd come in with him if he'd go back in the car and get her valise, because if she's in there with him she can't watch it. So he went on back there. And that was when Mr. Fireman, that had lit on his head and been knocked out for a second, jumped up almost under her feet from where he was laying on the side of the track, and began yelling at the top of his lungs to the people in the passenger cars that train-robbers have stole the engine and they're holding up the train. She didn't wait then for any signal. She heaved her spike, and pretty near went head first off the baggage car when the first passenger car went up in the air, then banged down on the ties with a jerk that broke the coupling, then went slamming off to the ditch with the other three cars piling up behind it.

Then she made a mistake. If she had stayed outside where she was, maybe the mail clerk, what with the shooting, the cord, and all, would have figured the excitement was still up front. But she had it in her mind she was to get in with the baggage and lock the baggage man out if she could, and even if he was left behind in the wrecked passenger cars she still supposed that's what she ought to do. But the mail clerk saw her through his peephole, and did something he wasn't ever supposed to do. He came back there. "Young woman, what are you doing here?"

"They're robbing the passengers back there! They've cut the train, and there's a wreck. Can't you hear the people screaming?"

"I asked you what you're doing here."

"I came to warn you."

"Why didn't you warn the conductor?"

"I thought he was up here."

"Where's the baggage man?"

"I don't know."

He took a quick look out back, then ran back in his compartment, opened the door in the forward partition, and hollered at Caskie. In a second he, the Wells, Fargo man, and Caskie were all back there, and of course when Caskie saw her he fitted it all together, like he had before. "Trying it again, hey?"

"Go to hell, Caskie."

"The last time, though."

"You sure about that?"

"Yeah, I'm sure. And it's not going to be any legal hanging either, with maybe a reprieve at the last minute. You're going to get just what your deadshot friend up there gave George Brewer. You're going to get it and he's going to get it. You'll be given your chance to run, and then when you do I'm going to shoot you both, and get commended by the grand jury for doing my duty, just like he was. That's a little trick they got down in Mexico, and very good it is."

"That's what you think you're going to do."

"But first we need a little help."

He slapped her all over to see if she had a gun, but she didn't. I had figured these hombres were all fast on the draw, and for her to try to shoot with them was practically the same as suicide. So when he was satisfied, he turned her around so her back was to him, pinned her arms behind her, and began hiking her through the mail compartment up toward the front end door, the one he had opened for shooting purposes.

But me, up front in the cab, I didn't know about

222

any of that. When Caskie began to shoot, I ducked back of the drop gate, and I just caught one flash of the wreck, and heard some screaming, before I began to shoot back. And then there was some yelling back there in the baggage car, and Caskie ducked away, and the shooting stopped. I just had time to reload when I heard her scream, and then here they came, Caskie carrying her by her elbows, which he had bent behind her, and holding her in front, for a shield, so I couldn't shoot, while she screamed and kicked and tried to bite. But it wasn't himself he was screening. It was the mail clerk, who dropped on the floor out of range and began to screw down the brake. And to cover him the Wells, Fargo man got behind Caskie and began shooting at me over Morina's shoulder.

I kept low and crawled around and closed the throttle. If they were going to stop me anyway I might as well save steam. We slowed down, and as we were coming to a stop, I kept out of sight near the tender and dropped to the ground. The Wells, Fargo man kept shooting, each shot banging against the drop gate like a chunk on a wash boiler. I kept close under, near the wheels, and when they came

223

up even with me, instead of Morina being a screen I had a clear shot. The mail clerk was still screwing the brake, Caskie was too close to Morina, but the Wells, Fargo man, who was the only one shooting, was framed in the door. I dropped him with one shot. Caskie let go of Morina and reached for his gun and she tried to hold on to him. I told her to let go and she did and I drilled him through the heart. That left the mail clerk, but he was already flattened against the car with his hands up, hollering he's not armed, he's got no gun, for God's sake don't shoot because he can't do anything. I let him have it in the head, and he toppled over frontwards against the brake and then down the steps to the ground.

"Christ, are you all right?"

"I think so."

"What did he do to you?"

"Held me, that was all."

"We got to hurry."

After I threw the two dead men on the car to the ground beside the mail clerk, I took her with me

up to the cab. But before I could move I had to
throw on some wood, because the gauge was drop-
ping bad. Then I ran on down to where the horses
were, about a mile. They were in a willow grove
beside the river, with packs, saddles, and everything ready for her, and she had practiced a hundred times what she had to do. Then I ran down to
the ditch, filled my hat with mud, and climbed
back in the car for what was next. I wasn't going to
try to lift that iron box full of gold. In my pocket
I had powder, that she had sewed into a little silk
bag, and a couple of feet of fuse, and some caps. I
figured to bust it open and load the money into the
saddle bags direct. So I began shaping my mud.
But then I noticed two other boxes in there that
might have something in them, but what to do with
one charge of powder I didn't know. But at a time
like that your head goes like you were crazy. I
dragged them over to Caskie's box, and pushed the
three of them together, so two of them were end to
end and the other one jammed up to the joint, like
you lay bricks. Then I mud-capped the T, so my
shot would bear down on all three. I had just lit the
fuse and jumped clear when here she came, with

the horses. She hopped down, peeled down to the men's overalls she had under her dress, changed to riding boots, and put on a man's hat. She had just finished when she gave a scream. I wheeled with my gun out, but it wasn't a man she was screaming about. It was the train, with our gold on it. It was moving. It was only then I remembered, they sometimes have two mail clerks, and all the time I'd been mud-capping, the second man must have dropped out his side door and crept up the track to the locomotive.

She got to the steps of the baggage car first, and that was when we had the one piece of luck we had all morning. He was too anxious, and when he opened full throttle, stead of going ahead he spun his wheels and the car ran up on the coupling. She lifted the pin and the engine shot ahead like a colt in a meadow, once the wheels took hold. But then she began to say my name in a way that made me turn cold all over. Because in pulling the pin she lost her balance, and there she was, hanging over the rail by one hand, with the car rolling up on her. I didn't grab for her. If I dropped her she'd lose her legs. I ran up the steps and screwed down the

brake, fast. The car stopped. She dropped to the
ground and I caught her in my arms. And that was
when my mud-cap went off.

Catching those horses, where they broke for the
river when that powder went up with a roar, while
from Sacramento by now a train must be coming
with a posse to get us, and on its way to Folsom was
our locomotive that would be coming back with another posse soon, that was one hell of a ten minutes.
And yet I'll remember that sight, of the baggage car
spilling its inside out on the bank beside the track,
the little time I've got left to live. Because the mud-
cap busted the boxes all right, but it busted the car
floor too, and out on the dirt, in the morning sun-
shine, came a river of gold, as well as diamonds,
sapphires, rubies, and pearls that were in the other
two boxes I found. And I'll never forget the sight
of her, either, on her hands and knees clawing that
stuff into the bags, with a look on her face like she
was some harpy drinking blood. She was still on
her hands and knees, and her fingernails were running blood, when I finally had the horses and was

ready to go. I said something to her two or three times and she didn't answer, just kept on digging. Then I stooped down and put my head on the rail. I could hear a hum. "Come on."

"But there's more in the ditch."

"I said come on."

"Oh! There's a diamond!"

"Come on!"

14

It was one hell of a day and one hell of a night, because when we made camp around sundown we didn't have the Folsom posse headed, like I thought we would. They had us headed, because I could hear them talking to each other, off there in the hills, and there was no way we could pass them and get to the high country. That meant we had to double back by moonlight, cross the railroad and the river, and sneak away on the other side. But at last, just before dawn, we hit a clump of woods where we could lay up for the day, and at least it seemed like we might be safe. That was when she lay close to me, and said nothing for a while, like she was thinking, and then popped at me: "Roger."

"Yes, Morina."

"Why did you kill him?"

"I killed three of them."

"Yes, but that last one. The one you didn't have to kill. The one that kept saying he didn't have any gun. The mail clerk."

"He had seen us. He'd know us."

"Is that the only reason?"

"When we come right down to it, we don't know how much they know. The baggage man saw you, and probably the other mail clerk that stole our engine. But whether they know that you had anything to do with what was done, that we don't know."

"Yes we do."

"Why take chances?"

"The baggage man knows all there is to know, and he wasn't even on the car we stole. He was left behind. You didn't have to kill that man."

"At least, I thought I did."

"Roger, you're a liar."

"If so, why?"

"You killed him for me."

"If I did I wouldn't admit it."

"So we can have one more night, like that night

in the mine, when we first found out what living
could be like."

"It's morning."

"Then one more morning."

"Take your mouth away."

"Kiss me. . . . Kiss me again."

A week later we had worked around Folsom,
past Sonora, and up a river I figure to be the Stanislaus. The night of the first snow, day before yesterday, we bedded down in this charcoal-burner's
shack where I'm sitting here writing. She spent the
night by the fire, sorting out all those jewels, then
putting rings on every finger and every toe, pinning
broaches in her hair and every place she could find
to put one, then wrapping herself in the blankets
with me. Every place I touched her something stuck
me, but she just laughed and I had to laugh too it
was so comical. Then in the morning she thought
she heard dogs, and I went out to look. I got out my
gun and crept to a rock where I could see the whole
valley, and sure enough some men were circling
around down there, on horses, with dogs baying.

But then a deer shot out of a thicket, and they were after him. I had been trembling, because I'd had the feeling we had a good head start and could make it, and I hated it, that they'd get us now, when we had practically won out. I relaxed, and started to climb down.

A twig cracked behind me. I wheeled and fired. And before I even saw her, my wife, my love, my life, was sinking down in the snow, a red velvet wrapper around her, diamonds and jewels all over her fingers and hair, and a little smile on her face before her head fell over.

I've been sitting here, all day and all night and all day again, writing it down. Writing down how it came about that a boy that went to St. Anne's in Annapolis, and believed what he heard there, should turn into a traitor, a killer, and a thief. I don't know why. Falling in love with Morina, that had something to do with it. But Virginia City had something to do with it too. Maybe they were wrong about the devil. Maybe he didn't move out like they said he did. Maybe they just thought he did. Maybe

he found a new way to conjure. Maybe he found if
you give people everything they want, and nothing
they ought to have, that'll wind them up in hell, too.
Anyhow, for me it's all over. I could make Nevada,
and the river, and Mexico, if I tried. But I can't try.
I'm at the end of the plank. Other dogs will be
along soon, and they won't be chasing deer. They'll
be after me. But when they get here, I'll be out
there with her, where she's covered up from the
birds and wolves, in the snow, with the gold piled
up at my feet, and this story at my head.

Here they come.